INVASION OF THE
SPIRIT PEOPLE

INVASION OF THE
SPIRIT PEOPLE

Juan Pablo Villalobos

Translated by Rosalind Harvey

SHEFFIELD – LONDON – NEW YORK

And Other Stories
Sheffield – London – New York
www.andotherstories.org

Originally published in 2020 by Editorial Anagrama S. A., Barcelona, as *La invasión
del pueblo del espíritu*

First edition in English, 2022, And Other Stories

9 8 7 6 5 4 3 2 1

ISBN: 9781913505363
eBook ISBN: 9781913505370

Editor: Bill Swainson; Copy-editor: Gesche Ipsen; Proofreader: Sarah Terry;
Typesetter: Tetragon, London; Typefaces: Neue Swift and Verlag; Cover Design:
Elisa von Randow. Printed and bound by the CPI Group (UK) Ltd, Croydon, CRO 4YY.

A catalogue record for this book is available from the British Library.

And Other Stories gratefully acknowledge that our work is supported using public
funding by Arts Council England.

For my parents
For my children

We are alone.
JOSÉ ALFREDO JIMÉNEZ

We are not alone.
FOX MULDER

CONTENTS

1

This is the story of Gastón and of his best friend, Max; it is also the story of Kitten, Gastón's dog, and of Pol, Max's son. There are lots of other characters in this story, but we're going to accompany Gastón at all times, as if we were floating just behind him and had access to his feelings, his sensations, the flow of this thoughts. Basically, we're a bunch of prying busybodies; we'll have to be cautious, then, or else he might push us aside and put an end to our plan. Our plan is to reach the last page of this book (don't go thinking this is some kind of conspiracy), and this is why we must follow Gastón, in the present, until we reach the end. The present is here, here as we write and here as we read. Here. The place, too, the city in which the story unfolds, is here. On this page – no need to go looking for it further on. After all, time and space are the same thing. Our place is the time we are moving through; the present is our place of residence. The past we will gradually come to understand along the way, because it is the connection between the present and future. The past will be the finger that will turn the pages of this book.

Let's turn the page: the future is there.

2

They are alone in the empty restaurant, 13.8 billion years after the birth of our universe, watching a match played by the city team, the team for which the best footballer on Earth plays, and drinking a second beer at the bar; Gastón on the customers' side, with Kitten lying at his feet, dozing, and Max on the barman's side. It's a rustic wooden bar, painted green, which aims to imitate those from Max's native land, although the peppers that decorate it are more reminiscent of those from the Near East; the carpenter Max hired was, in fact, Near Eastern, and he turned out to be a good carpenter – efficient and reliable – but useless when it came to vernacular styles from other lands. The metal shutters at the entrance are down and there is a sign saying CLOSED FOR THE HOLIDAYS, which is how Max plans to avoid having to explain things to his customers and local residents.

'What if we bought the premises?' Gastón asks Max.

This is Max, or what is left of him, if we pay attention to how Gastón feels when he looks at his friend. Max, his shoulders hunched and his eyes permanently lowered ever since he discovered the multicoloured sweetie game on his phone. He's going through a rough patch, Max; first his son had to go and live far away for work, and then he lost his restaurant, or rather was swindled out of it. The landlord sold it behind his back, taking advantage of the rental agreement having expired, without giving him a chance to renegotiate. Since then, Max has shut himself away in the building that is both the restaurant and his home; this arrangement, which, years ago, was a practical solution – living in the same building as the restaurant, which occupies the ground floor – now helps facilitate his monastic routine. In the morning he comes down from the third floor, spends the day in the restaurant not doing anything, and goes back up when he's finished (and since not doing anything is an activity that can easily spiral out of control, he tends to go back up pretty late, generally in the early hours of the morning). He has just a few days left to hand over the premises, and the only thing he has done, the only decision he has made, is not to open the place up again to customers.

Inside, it smells of rancid, fried sunflower oil, the topped-up, reheated oil in which there remains perhaps a billionth of a litre of the original oil into which Max threw a few triangles of corn tortilla for the first time almost thirty years ago to make a plate of nachos with avocado salsa. Every TV in the place is switched on, including the huge screen in the dining area, because there's a system that controls them all simultaneously. It must be possible to operate them independently, but that would involve working out how, asking the technician who installed them, or racking his brains to remember, and this is one of the many things that Max ought to be doing but continues to put off, as if there were no cut-off date, no deadline on the calendar, not the last day of the month. The volume on the TVs is down; we are missing the strident voice of the commentator, his litany of words pouring out in the native language, and the general hubbub of customers drinking on their feet, crowding around the bar, for it to be just any old night.

'I haven't got any money,' Max replies.

'I've got savings,' Gastón says; 'we could go into business together.'

'I'm tired,' Max replies, without lifting his head, staring at the screen of his phone instead of the game. 'I don't want to talk about this.'

Gastón knows that when Max says he's tired he means that he's already written off this and other options. Rents in the neighbourhood have gone up so much that he'd be forced to pay almost double for new premises; he could move to a cheaper location, although then he would lose his regular customers and have to start all over again from zero, something that seems deplorable to him at his age (Max is fifty-five years old, one year younger than Gastón).

The screens show that the best footballer on Earth has stopped running. He is leaning forwards, his hands on his knees, and spitting, or perhaps vomiting. The game continues, although the cameras remain on him, as if the ball were merely an accessory or the aim of the game were to suffer some kind of ailment.

'What's wrong with him?' Gastón asks, addressing the air, addressing an interlocutor who is not outside his head, addressing himself, this page, us.

He picks up the remote control and turns the sound up to hear the commentator say that in the land where the best footballer on Earth was born they're reporting that he's afraid, that he has anxiety attacks, and that this is why he is incapable of leading his side to a World Cup win. Meanwhile, the city team is passing the ball back and forth, making its opponents dizzy, waiting for the hero to regain his composure. Gastón turns the volume back down again. All at once, Max emerges from the daze he's in, leans over the bar and holds some nachos out to the dog. Kitten flattens his ears and his eyes fill with tears; it's the same expression he makes whenever he's sick on Gastón's sofa or his bed. We assume that he's trying to say yes, but he is a dog. A dog in pain. Last week, Gastón took him to the vet's after finding a lump on his chest. It was a mass of abnormal cells, malignant ones, which had already spread through his whole body.

'When does the treatment start?' Max asks, plunging his hand into a giant bag of nachos. He walks around the bar in slow motion, places a handful of fried tortillas on the floor, in front of the dog's muzzle, and kisses the top of his head.

Gastón replies with an insult that shocks us, an insult that mentions Max's mother, or rather, not exactly *his* mother; it's one of those rhetorical insults so common in Max's native land and which Gastón has adopted as his own after so many years alongside his friend.

Is Gastón an irascible guy? Another one of those angry maniacs so common in the history of literature? Let's hope not. We're tired of stories about men with chips on their shoulders, fed up with glorifying resentment and frustration. No, it's OK; now we understand what's going on: someone has just scored a goal against the city's team.

3

They say that the Far Easterners have been buying up everything in the neighbourhood. Cafés, bars, restaurants, traditional businesses like haberdashers or corner shops, which they turn into budget bazaars selling household goods for a few cents. Gastón interrogates Yu, the Far Easterner from the budget bazaar on the same corner as the restaurant (Max has refused to give him the details). But this time it's not the Far Easterners; our assumptions were too hasty. They are from the East, but not the Far East, the Near East.

'The same ones who opened up the new greengrocer's around the corner,' Yu explains, making a superhuman effort to pronounce the r's in the word 'greengrocer's'.

Gastón makes his way over there. But they're not from the Near East, either; they are North Easterners.

4

The North Easterner in the greengrocer's insists that Gastón properly identify himself if he wants to talk business; he needs to know where he comes from and what he does, in order to activate the territorial and trade-related codes of trust, or of distrust. It is not easy to determine where Gastón comes from; his skin, darker than that of the Peninsulars, his cheeks, which are broad, his almost grey eyes, and the abundance of hair on his ears, which, more than a physical attribute, is a lycanthropic sign of premature ageing, all produce a peculiar visual effect, resistant to classification. The way he speaks doesn't help, either; the strange accent with which he intones the colonising language after so many years of living here (more than thirty), and the vocabulary, which is a blend of his own quaint lexicon with that of the Peninsula, with that of Max, and with sayings and expressions taken from the indigenous language.

'I'm from the Southern Cone,' Gastón says. 'Southern Conish. I have the market garden up behind the Historic Park.'

'On the hill?' the North Easterner asks, in surprise.

'It's good land,' Gastón replies; 'I just need to clear it and put some terraces in. If you want to come along one day, I'll show you round; we can have a beer.'

The North Easterner asks him if he supplies the shops owned by his rivals. The two men are surrounded by crates of fruit and vegetables and yet Gastón feels out of place, a farmer in an umbrella factory. The merchandise gleams in the light of the pre-spring morning, too clean, too brightly coloured, everything waxed or wrapped in plastic. There are almost no traces of earth, no smells. The label stuck to each one of the crates indicates the thousands of miles of transport by sea or by land, from enormous plots worked by semi-slave labour in the South Eastern or South Western parts of the Earth.

Gastón explains that his is a small plot, that his customers are restaurants and individuals, that he grows herbs, fruit and exotic vegetables, the stuff that gets called 'gourmet' or 'ethnic', and that for many years now he has in fact grown the peppers that Max uses to make the sauces for the nachos and stews from his native land.

'And you can live off that?' the North Easterner asks.

It's a good question, characteristic of someone with enough economic nous to understand that agriculture is only a viable business as long as the volume of production increases. Gastón replies that it's enough to get by, that he is capable of looking after the plot on his own and that he has few expenses and no family. Nonetheless, this does not explain his having enough money to buy the restaurant, but this train of thought appears to be one the North Easterner does not immediately engage in, or, if he does, he keeps it to himself.

At this moment, Kitten, who accompanies Gastón wherever he goes, starts whimpering and writhing around on the floor. These episodes began after his illness was detected; in all likelihood it's a coincidence, even though we are tempted to attribute it to some perceptive power on the part of the dog, as if the diagnosis had stimulated his pain receptors. Gastón bends down to try and soothe the animal; this time, the episode lasts only a few seconds, Kitten grows calm again and remains lying on the floor, fearing that if he moves the pain might come back; he stays so motionless that it looks more like superstition than a reflex. In his doggy logic of cause and effect, when he lies down, the pain goes away.

'What's wrong with him?' the North Easterner asks.

'He has a genetic mutation,' Gastón replies. 'It's just been diagnosed.'

All at once he grows emotional, his cheeks burn and his tear ducts receive the alert: here come the sadness hormones. The North Easterner realises what's going on.

'It won't work,' he says.

Gastón replies that he doesn't understand.

'If this is some kind of negotiation tactic, making me feel sorry for your dog,' the North Easterner explains. 'I can't sell. The restaurant's for my brother – he's moving here with his family and we need the land the premises are on to apply for the visa.'

He explains that in his native land there is no work and no soil to cultivate, that the soil was devastated in the last border war between the North Easterners from the north and the North Easterners from the south, the war in which his wife, the mother of his daughter, died. He says all this coldly, perhaps so Gastón doesn't think that he's raising the stakes in the commiseration competition; and then the North Easterner turns his head and looks behind him, towards the door leading to the back room of the shop, where a little girl has appeared, as if to prove he isn't lying. She must be three or four years old; more likely just turned three very recently, because if she were older she would be at nursery at this hour. She comes over slowly, dragging her feet and wrestling with her shyness, until she reaches the spot on the floor where Kitten is lying. She says something to her father in a language we don't understand.

'She wants to know what the dog is called,' the North Easterner says.

Gastón tells her, repeating it three times, emphasising each syllable distinctly, assuming that this way it's more likely that the little girl will understand him. The North Easterner seems confused by the contradiction in the dog's name, but he says nothing, perhaps because he thinks he has misunderstood (this assumption is ours). The little girl, meanwhile, sees no contradiction; after all, it was another child – Pol, Max's son – who many years ago gave the dog this name.

'And what about you?' Gastón asks.

Her father replies that she is called Varushka. The little girl bends down to look closely at the dog and says something.

'She's asking if she can stroke him,' the North Easterner translates.

Gastón says yes, that the dog loves children. The North Easterner performs his role as interpreter. The child sits down on the floor and runs her right hand gently over Kitten's head, over and over, all the while repeating, over and over again, a sweet, short phrase, like a little song, like the magic spell in a fairy tale.

'She says that he's a very pretty wolf,' the North Easterner translates.

5

As soon as he wakes up, Gastón makes a video call to Pol, Max's son. Pol finished his Biology degree and, after a period of inactivity alarmingly similar to that of the microbes that were the focus of his thesis, got a job with a team of scientists researching life in extreme conditions. The work compels him to live in a frozen place far away, above the snow line, in the Tundra, six hours ahead towards the East of the West where Gastón and Max live. It seems like an exciting job, and it is, but the contract is only for a year and its extension depends on the research institute receiving further funding. Indeed, Pol's salary is paid not by the university, but by a group of investors who are covering a portion of the institute's budget.

'He doesn't even get up to let me in,' Gastón tells Pol. 'It's lucky he gave me a set of keys for emergencies. He's got to hand over the premises at the end of the month and he's done nothing. There's food just rotting away in the fridges.'

He tries to gauge Pol's reaction through the screen of his phone; we watch over his shoulder: more than sad or concerned, the lad looks scared, although this might be for some other reason. Or perhaps this expression doesn't represent a state of mind at all but rather one of the body; perhaps it's the cold (Pol is wearing a gigantic coat). He doesn't look very much like Max – hardly at all, in fact; at most in the signs of a receding hairline already visible at his temples, and we can't be sure that he's inherited this from his father, since baldness is multigenetic. If it weren't for the fact that Gastón is talking to him, it would be hard for us to guess that this is Pol. But since we do know this, we can try to picture his mother, in comparison to Max: darker-skinned, nose a little more snub, lips slightly thinner, and that slightly wonky set of teeth in the jaw, as if they were false and might clatter out at the first sign of a laugh.

Is this what Pol's mother looked like? We have no way of knowing, and in fact it doesn't matter, because the truth does not reside in an image but rather in the process of imagining, in what happens between mind and matter, in how we tell this story. In fact, Gastón barely remembers her (she and Max never lived together as a couple), and only saw her a few times when Pol first started school and he, Gastón, would give his friend a hand with the logistics of shared custody, that tangle of timetables, changes of clothes, rucksacks and lunch boxes, shortly before she had the car crash while on holiday in her native land, the same place Max comes from.

Pol is shivering, and we feel sure that, if the connection were better, we'd be able to hear his teeth chattering.

'Do you not have any heating out there?' Gastón asks him.

'I'm at the university,' Pol replies. 'I've come out into the corridor so no one hears us.'

'Can anyone understand us in the Tundra?'

'There are people from all over here, quite a few from the Southern Cone, some from the Peninsula.'

'What's the temperature there today?'

'Right now? Minus twenty-five.'

According to what Pol has told him, it could be far worse: there are days, in this period of the year when winter's grip is particularly hard and spring is in no hurry, when the thermometer displays ten degrees lower than that.

'Where are you?' Pol asks. 'I can hardly see you.'

Gastón replies that he's at home, sitting in the living room, and asks Pol to wait while he turns on the light, because the Earth hasn't turned sufficiently yet to bring him out of the gloom. He leaves his phone on the coffee table and gets up, and we seize the opportunity to move our gaze away from the device's screen and take a look around, at the solid pieces of old, heavy furniture, from back when there was real wood, from back when there were still forests and we chopped down trees with abandon. We also see the twentieth-century curtains and tablecloth, made from industrially produced polyester, and the dinner service with its gilt edges, displayed in the cabinet. It's an old dinner service, which belonged to the woman who owns the house, but it's not antique: it's merely old and chipped, like all the things here, the remains of another life that Gastón had no problem stepping into when he moved in, without making them his own, without adjusting them at all, like a traveller who planned on stopping here just for one night. Many years ago, the owner had to be admitted to an old people's home and the family put the house up for rent; Gastón installed himself there just as a son of hers would have done if she'd had one. The woman died quite some time ago, and since then the agency has been transferring the rent money to a niece who doesn't live in the city. There is a bedroom, a room that serves as a utility room, a kitchen and a bathroom, but not one photo, no picture frame, not a trace of the four or five romantic partners Gastón has had, nor of any family or ancestors, as if he has just popped up out of nowhere, out of thin air, although, in actual fact, he came from the same place we all come from, from the womb of a mother (who died when he was a teenager), from a land he felt excluded from because it always seemed alien to him, a quirk of fate he corrected by leaving as soon as possible.

'We've got to do something about your dad,' Gastón insists, when he picks up the phone again, going back to their conversation.

Pol tells him that it'll pass, that his father will grow tired of being shut up indoors, that he's grieving for the restaurant but is ultimately a man of action who doesn't know how to stay still. That he's been working non-stop for a long time and deserves a bit of a break.

'Can you not come home?' Gastón asks. 'I'm sure that would cheer him up, he really misses you.'

'Not right now,' Pol replies. 'It's not a good time. We're on the verge of something really big. I can't tell you what it is; there are confidentiality clauses, you know how it is. But I'll come home as soon as I can, I promise.'

Gastón watches on the screen as Pol looks off to one side, and hears him say something in a language we don't understand.

'I've got to go,' Pol says.

He pauses so as to soften the goodbye, so as not to seem rude.

'How's Kitten?' he asks.

'He asks after you every day,' Gastón replies, so that he doesn't have to talk about the dog's health.

'Give him a kiss from me,' Pol says. 'And look after Dad, please. I'll be checking in.' He gestures goodbye with his free gloved hand and then, before hanging up, remembers something. He asks Gastón if he knows what's going on with his grandfather, which surprises Gastón, not just due to the sudden shift in the conversation, but because this is a topic they don't usually speak about. Gastón and Max's father have only ever spent time together during the occasional visits of the old man, who lives in the opposite direction in both space and time, nine hours behind Gastón and Max, fifteen hours behind Pol, on the edge of the western part of the West, in the Peninsula of one of the ex-Colonies. There have been very few visits – perhaps four or five in the thirty years he has known Max.

'Is something up?' Gastón asks.

'Hasn't my dad told you?' Pol replies.

Gastón imagines it must be some sort of health issue; Pol's grandfather isn't that old – he can't be much more than seventy – but this is an age when news often has a finality to it.

'Is he ill?' he asks.

'No, it's not that – Dad'll explain,' Pol replies, and he hangs up.

6

Gastón would rather not ask Max, but a simple internet search is enough to figure out what Pol is referring to. The newspapers from that other Peninsula, the one in the ex-Colonies where Pol's grandfather lives, are talking about a committee being set up to look into the accounts of the council where Max's father was minister for public works in the previous government. The most recent article says that his whereabouts are currently unknown. There is speculation that he may have made use of the fact that his ancestors were Peninsulars, from the colonising Peninsula, to cross borders with that passport without being identified.

Max is the eldest in a line of children that, as Gastón calculates now, without being certain, must be approaching a dozen between legitimate and alternative offspring (Max is the lucky first child on that second list). He was conceived when his parents were still teenagers; he is what we would call 'a sin of youth' if this were a romantic novel, but here we will say that he was the product of a reckless act caused by an overdose of happiness hormones.

Shortly after they met, on one of those nights out from his early days in the city, Max asked his new friend what he was running away from. Expressed like that, it sounded a little over the top. No longer was this the period of exiles from dictatorships in the ex-Colonies of the Far West; nowadays, people moved for work or family reasons, out of economic necessity or the desire for a better life (this 'nowadays' refers to the time of that conversation, thirty years ago). Or, as Gastón tried to explain to Max, out of a sense of inadequacy or incompatibility; because of the certainty that one did not belong to the land where one was born.

'We're all running away from someone,' we hear Gastón remember Max say.

It wasn't the time or the place for one of Gastón's philosophical explanations, his booze-drenched strings of gibberish about how putting some distance between yourself and the land of your birth was a condition of freedom, his lengthy spiel on territorial relocation as rebirth, as an opportunity to destroy one's past identity, to be someone new or to never again be no one in particular.

'We're saying the same thing,' we hear Max say in Gastón's recollection. 'We're all running away from our fathers.'

'But my father was already dead when I decided to come over here,' Gastón recalls.

'Even worse,' Max says, in the memory; 'that means you've come here to look for him.'

7

In the surgery's reception, after the vet has explained the results of the test, after he has destroyed all of Gastón's hopes and told him that he shouldn't prolong the dog's suffering unnecessarily, he gives Gastón an envelope filled with documents. It's the animal's diagnosis, the X-rays, the prescriptions, the instructions. The papers weigh heavy like a sentence in Gastón's hands.

The receptionist is waiting for Gastón to choose the date when he will bring Kitten in to 'carry out the procedure'. These were the words the vet used, and which the receptionist now repeats. What do these words have to do, Gastón thinks, with the death of his companion?

'Does the day after tomorrow suit you?' the receptionist presses him.

Gastón pretends someone is ringing him, holds his phone up to his right ear, makes an apologetic face, tugs on the lead with his left hand to drag Kitten away, and escapes from the clinic.

8

He goes to the estate agent he rents his house from to set out the issue. His idea is to buy another premises somewhere in the vicinity for a roughly equivalent price, so that he can propose an exchange to the North Easterner. A very young agent comes over to serve him, a boy who seems familiar – he may have been a classmate of Pol's at primary school, or perhaps had football lessons with him, although Gastón can't be completely sure. The agent is dressed in a cheap suit, a uniform really, a disguise to cover up his precarious status, and a ridiculous bottle-green tie he is obliged to wear in order to match the office decor and the company's corporate image.

He carries out a detailed database search, which takes nearly half an hour, but, after ruling out various options, there is nothing. The agent explains, by way of an apology, what Gastón knows he avoided telling him at the start, something the agent already knew (and that Gastón did, too), but his work consists of simulating such searches, of waiting for a miracle to occur. The miracle is called 'new listing in the agency's database'.

'The market's pretty buoyant right now,' the agent says, finally. 'And it's worse in this area, because it's trendy at the moment.'

'That's what they say,' Gastón replies, thinking that part of the strategy for how to buoy up the market still further is the very pantomime they've just performed. The agent offers Gastón his card, a brochure and the company magazine, then checks his details and promises he will call if something with the features Gastón is looking for turns up. Gastón gets to his feet and pulls on Kitten's lead, but the agent stops him.

'If you ever think about selling that market garden of yours, do let me know,' he says, changing the subject. 'I don't know how the land is designated up there, but you're sitting on an absolute gold mine.'

Gastón is now convinced that the agent is indeed a friend, or an acquaintance at the very least, of Pol's. He nods his head in response, nothing more. He is not offended by the kid interfering like this, nor does he feel obliged to respond. He knows this is what everyone assumes he will have to do so he can retire. Getting planning permission for a change of use of the land was something Max always used to speak to him about, the old Max, the pragmatic man of action with two feet firmly planted on the ground.

'Can I ask you a question?' the agent asks.

'Go ahead,' Gastón says, trying once more to remember what the relationship is between the agent and Pol, where he knows the kid from.

'Is it really such good business, the market garden? So good you've got enough savings to buy a premises at this price, I mean? Don't take it the wrong way – I'm just curious. My grandparents emigrated from the countryside, from the South, because they were slowly starving to death.'

'It produces a fair bit,' Gastón replies, 'but I've got a bit of inheritance, too.'

'That's what I thought,' replies the agent.

Immediately he regrets blurting this out, a rude phrase that creates an awkwardness in the atmosphere, and hurriedly picks up his phone from the desk.

'Did you see the video Pol posted?' he asks, unlocking the device and swiping the index finger of his right hand over the screen.

Gastón tells him he doesn't use social media and then asks him where he knows Pol from.

'From the Square of the Women,' the agent says.

That's why Gastón doesn't remember him properly: his was one more face in the mad dance of small children running after balls or riding their bikes. Every afternoon for years, Gastón would go to pick Pol up from school at five o'clock, with the boy's afternoon snack; Max couldn't do it, because that was the time he had to get the restaurant ready for the evening service. On Mondays and Wednesdays Gastón would take Pol to football practice, and the rest of the week he would take him to play in the Square of the Revolutionary Women (which people generally shorten to the Square of the Women), halfway between Pol's school and the restaurant. Then, at around 7 p.m., he would drop him off at the restaurant, where they would be welcomed by Max placing a beer, a hibiscus flower juice and a bowl of nachos with avocado salsa on the bar in front of them.

Eventually the agent finds the video and passes his phone to Gastón. We see Pol in the snow – the ice, really. In his right hand he has a phone which he holds up to the camera – the camera of another phone which one of his colleagues must be holding, we imagine – to show the temperature displayed on an app: −32°C. Then the camera moves closer to Pol's face as he squeezes his eyes tightly shut, his face growing red, until two tears appear at his lower lids and then, before they can roll down his face, freeze immediately. Pol lifts his gloved hand up to his eyes and tries to wipe away the two little drops of ice. He laughs because the gloves mean he can't conclude the little performance.

9

Kitten has another attack, this time in the street, just as Gastón and the dog are walking past the window of the Far Eastern budget bazaar. Yu witnesses the scene from behind the counter and hurries out to help. Kitten soon stops whimpering, but he does not get up. Yu asks Gastón what's wrong with him. His two children, a girl and a boy of around seven and five, we reckon, have also come out of the shop.

'Is he in pain?' the little boy asks in the native language.

Gastón says yes, that he's an old dog, and is ill. The little girl sits down on the flowery pavement tiles to keep Kitten company, and when she moves her hand as if to stroke him Yu shouts at her in a language we don't understand, in one of the numerous languages spoken in the Far East. We don't understand the language, but we can hazard a guess at the general sense of Yu's shout: don't touch the dog without asking; or just: don't touch it at all – perhaps worried that Kitten might react badly due to the pain he's in.

The girl gets up and both children wander off before Gastón can intervene in her favour, or realise that what Yu actually shouted at them both was an order to get back inside the shop.

'Is there a cure?' Yu asks.

Gastón stands staring at Kitten as if he hasn't understood this question, either, as if we have to interpret it. Yu tells him that when he was a boy he had a dog that fell ill and had to be put to sleep; he says that it was done by a sedatoress, that sedatoresses use traditional medicine to alleviate pain and to put those who are suffering to sleep for ever. He says all this in other words, using the colonising language in a way that reveals another structure of thought. Gastón repeats the words in his head; we hear him do it, imitating Yu's soft r's, which makes the words even sweeter, removing them even further from the vet's technical, bookkeeping vocabulary. He asks Yu if he knows of any sedatoresses here in the city, and Yu lights a cigarette as if the tobacco were going to help him think or remember, but then shakes his head no and says that this was a long time ago, in his native land. Gastón takes his wallet from the back pocket of his trousers and pulls out a business card. It has his full name, his phone number, his email address and the address of the market garden. He asks Yu to let him know if he hears something or has any idea about how to locate a sedatoress.

The two men lapse into silence, watching Kitten, his hesitant breathing. He's still not quite calm yet, and Gastón prefers to wait before setting off again. He wonders if he should make use of the situation, which seems propitious, to interrogate Yu, ask for his help. He ponders the best way to do this, chooses the words before opening his mouth. Eventually, he makes up his mind and asks Yu if they have a particular estate agent that manages the purchase of premises for them. Gastón uses the plural form of 'you', a form that, in the Peninsula, suggests formal or ceremonial use, but which is the most commonly used form of the word in most of the ex-Colonies of the Far West.

'We?' Yu replies. 'Whether "we" have one?'

Gastón has fallen into his own trap. Concerned with not linking his question to Yu's background, with not mentioning the land in the Far East from which Yu, his family and his compatriots, owners of the Far Eastern budget bazaars in the area, emigrated, he has committed a greater offence: segregating him; using this plural form of 'you' places them apart, separates them, distinguishes them, groups them together. Yu notices Gastón's embarrassment. Gastón has gone red and his instinctive reaction is to apologise, but he doesn't do this, because he thinks that this would entail a double humiliation, for him and for Yu. But Yu appears amused.

'Do "we" have an agent to manage the purchase of premises for "us"?' he says again, this time without trying to hide his pronunciation, without making any particular effort with the 'r' sound, turning it into the 'l' that indicates the phonetic stereotype one expects from Far Easterners when speaking the colonising language.

He lets out a loud laugh, whether genuine or forced we can't tell, throws the end of his cigarette down onto the pavement, claps Gastón on the shoulder and goes back into the bazaar.

10

Kitten's suffering has a name, one of those hard-to-pronounce names that diseases tend to have. We don't want to name it here, just as there are other things we don't name, some because they aren't important, others because by refusing to name them they seem even more ominous to us.

At the vet's, Gastón was told that Kitten would no longer really be able to exert himself, but that he should not resign himself to seeing his pet just lying on the floor, and should insist on taking him for short walks. Not moving might mean that the animal's muscles will atrophy for good, they said. Atrophy. Now we've dirtied the page. Anyway. The long walks at dusk and first thing in the morning, in the interval between the first chores of the day and breakfast, come to an end. Now Gastón sticks to what's essential, to covering the distance that separates the market garden from Max's restaurant, from his house, from the supermarket where Gastón always does the shopping because they don't make him leave Kitten tied up at the entrance.

We'd like to go inside Kitten's head, to find out if he realises what's happening to him, how he interprets what awaits him, to disprove the belief that we have superiority over the other living beings that inhabit the Earth; once in there, we could also document the catalogue of smells in the neighbourhood, updated on each walk, but let's not try and con anyone. No one can go inside a dog's head. We must be satisfied with Gastón, we've got more than enough with this responsibility. We were given a special power to write this story; let's not abuse it.

Gastón looks for a local sedatoress on the internet; he tries to ignore everything that does not lead to his specific goal, a local telephone number or an email address, but he fails. On his phone, he scrolls through pages that eventually lead him down dead ends. Ads for good luck charms. Meditation courses. Treatments from the Far East and the Near. Detoxing by hypnosis. When a virus alert pops up after he clicks on one particular link, he concludes he will have to turn to more traditional methods.

He calls one of the many businesses in the city selling spiritual products and explains the situation to the man who answers the phone. In a maternal voice, he informs Gastón that his business specialises in healing crystals, and he is sorry but can't help. Gastón rings another of these shops. The woman who picks up sounds suspicious, asks if Gastón is from the police. She then hangs up, giving Gastón no time to try and deny this.

The mention of the police unsettles Gastón, although he reassures himself that the woman's wariness has to do with the activities of her business and not with the fact that his request is so strange that it seems like a crime. The phone rings. It's the man from the first shop. He tells Gastón he's just thought of a way to solve his problem.

'Talk to the Peninsular Association of Traditional Healers,' he explains. 'They'll put you on the right track.'

Gastón writes down the number the man from the first shop reads out to him in his maternal voice, says goodbye, thanking him for his kindness, then hangs up and immediately rings the number. It rings three times then goes to an answerphone. He tries a few more times over the next couple of hours, with exactly the same result. He ends up leaving a brief message, asking them to call him back urgently.

Although it might look like the opposite is true, Gastón does not believe in Far Eastern philosophies, nor is he seeking them out because tragedy has weakened his spirit. What he wants is to keep Kitten company in these moments, to not leave his side and for everything to happen without altering the dog's routine, schedule or familiar places. He wants the sedatoress to come to the market garden, which is where he plans to bury Kitten.

11

The lawyer comes looking for Gastón at the market garden. It wasn't hard to find him; the city is big, but the neighbourhood is like a village – by quizzing two or three people, even at random, you can locate just about anyone. He's managed to get into the garden because the gate is always unlocked, but has chosen not to move too far away from where his motorbike is parked. Gastón greets him on the defensive; he doesn't like visits in general, never mind unexpected ones. Many years ago, when Pol was little, Max used to come by this place every Saturday or Sunday to have an early evening beer in the shade of the carob tree or the tool shed. It was nice to chat, but they had to take care to watch Pol, because as soon as their attention drifted he would start pulling up potatoes. Gastón is not going to offer the lawyer a beer, but he does at least lead him over to the other shady area in the market garden, the little lean-to Gastón has put up by the gate to shelter the delivery van.

'I hear you're interested in getting your friend's restaurant back,' the lawyer says. He has a thick accent, from the Central Plateau, or it seems so to Gastón, who isn't exactly an expert in the regional peculiarities of the Peninsula (we aren't, either). He says that he represents a group of residents and traders who have come together to stand up to the invasion the neighbourhood is undergoing.

'It is an invasion,' he insists, 'and if we don't do anything, soon it'll just be budget bazaars run by Far Easterners, corner shops run by Near Easterners, and greengrocers' run by North Easterners.'

He gesticulates as he says this, waving his hands and scowling to accentuate the dramatic nature of the matter. The truth is that the man is darker-skinned than he really ought to be if he wants his little speech to have more credibility. Gastón explains, in case the man isn't aware, that he and Max also come from elsewhere. And that the restaurant in question used to serve traditional food from the land where his friend was born.

'That's different,' the lawyer replies. 'We have a shared past, we speak the same language. Where are you from?'

'The Southern Cone,' Gastón says.

'You see?' the lawyer exclaims. 'Our people are similar, we've never forgotten the Colonies. We're in this together.'

The lawyer looks past Gastón, towards the terraces of the market garden, over to where the carob tree stands out against the horizon. For a second, Gastón fantasises about the tree reaching out one of its branches and curling it around the lawyer's throat to shut him up, but the carob has sweet sap; if Gastón had wanted a tree to defend his land he ought to have planted one with bitter berries, or a prickly bush of some sort – a wild olive, say.

'My family's from the countryside,' the lawyer says in a dreamy voice. 'All this reminds me of summers in my childhood. Are those elongated onions?' he asks, pointing towards the bed, which does, in fact, contain a crop of elongated onions.

After Gastón replies in the affirmative, the lawyer moves his outstretched arm over to the neighbouring bed, where four rows of bushes with spear-shaped leaves can be seen.

'And over there, in that bit of earth?' he asks, as if he were a child on a school trip.

'They're . . . a kind of earth vegetable,' Gastón replies, evasively.

'Ah . . . from which part of the Earth?' the lawyer replies.

'Ask them,' says Gastón, 'I imagine they'd tell you they're from this earth right here.'

'Are they from the same part of the Earth as where you're from?' the lawyer insists, suddenly sounding more interested. He asks him if these are the potatoes that the best footballer on Earth likes, the famous earth vegetables from the same part of the Earth as the best footballer on Earth, and says that he recalls having read something in the newspaper saying that he couldn't live without them, that he had them grown in a local market garden, and perhaps Gastón is the one who grows them for him? Gastón realises his mistake and interrupts the lawyer to steer the conversation in a different direction (he promised the owner of the Southern Cone restaurant who recommended him to the best footballer on Earth's father that he would never tell anyone he was the supplier, and this has meant, on more than one occasion, turning down interviews with the sports press, which had a childish desire to see in the nostalgic craving for this ingredient something talismanic, the source of the hero of the city's superpowers); he says that he thinks there's been a misunderstanding. That he does want to help Max, but has nothing against the Far Easterners or the North Easterners.

'Or against lawyers from the country, either,' he adds, with kindly sarcasm, an unlikely combination which lets us see that, while Gastón might be a bit of a recluse, he's certainly not a misanthrope.

Kitten lets out a whimper of pain from wherever he is lying, somewhere near the shed where Gastón keeps his tools. The lawyer realises that this is the pretext Gastón will use to excuse himself.

'If you give me your number I'll let you know what's going on in the neighbourhood,' the lawyer says. 'It's important we remain united.'

He explains that he's started an e-newsletter that is sent via the instant messaging app everyone uses. Gastón gives the lawyer his number, to put an end to the discussion, and because he knows, in any case, that the man will have no problem getting hold of it. The lawyer turns to look behind him, confirms that no one has stolen his motorbike, and walks off.

12

It isn't a science programme, it's a national television strategy to glorify territoriality. They go all over the world visiting people from the Peninsula, people suffering from nostalgic distortion as a result of how far away they have moved in space. Gastón only sees it online a few days after it's shown, because a customer told him that the latest episode had been filmed in the Tundra and that Pol was in it. We would have liked to see him on a bigger screen, get a little snack together, some olives, maybe have a beer, but Gastón watches it on his phone during a break from working, sitting in the shade of the tool shed's veranda, his earphones in, and we have to go inside his head in order to listen.

The part where Pol appears, along with three other Peninsular colleagues, is filmed in a lab. Gastón recognises it from the photos Pol sent him a few months ago, when he'd just started his new job. An older man with an accent from the south is explaining, in a muddled sort of way, the investigations they currently have on the go. He talks of bacteria capable of pausing and remaining in suspended animation, of microorganisms that survive despite their metabolism stopping altogether. He says that there is life that does not depend on solar energy, that the presence of methane is a sign of biological life and that these investigations might help to discover life on other planets. The presenter tries to make a funny comment about flying saucers, but the older man doesn't even let him finish.

'Life is a chemical system capable of Darwinian evolution,' he says sternly. 'Everything else is literature.'

The disdain with which the older man pronounces the word 'literature' offends us, but Gastón doesn't even notice (he is not a man of letters, of books, does not read novels). Another of the scientists steps in to smooth over this little outburst, explaining how life has been found where it should not, in theory, exist, after they drilled more than 3,000 feet down into the ice, in a subglacial lake that had been isolated by ice layers dating back over 400,000 years. The third scientist has the most didactic tone; he treats the presenter and, by extension, the viewers, like children. Slowly, pausing to allow us to digest the information, he says that these organisms are called extremophiles.

'These are organisms that flourish in conditions that are intolerable for higher forms of life,' he concludes.

Strange as it might seem, this all feels familiar to Gastón: it was the subject of Pol's thesis and of many of their conversations while he was writing it; even so, Pol has until now remained in the background on the screen, right at the back, in fact; he is the youngest and certainly the least experienced, and so is not called upon to say anything. They then move to the university cafeteria, where they show the food they eat in the Tundra (fish jellies and fermented dairy products), and list all the dishes from the Peninsula that they miss. The older man is the most compelling: he lists cured pork products in a trembling voice, a real tour de force.

Only then does the presenter notice Pol's silence and ask him how it feels to be part of a group of Peninsulars working on such a momentous project for science. The camera zooms in on a surprised Pol, who would have been content with his role as a minor extra.

'I don't know,' Pol says. 'There are researchers from all over the Earth here.'

The presenter seems to think that Pol is shy, and tries again to get a response out of him; he congratulates him, says that he and his fellow researchers are a source of pride for those back in his homeland. Although this is a demagogic message, Gastón does feel proud again, as on so many other occasions, not because they are from the same country, but because he believes that Pol's interest in biology, even if he has never admitted as much, has something to do with him, Gastón, and his market garden.

'Which part of the Peninsula are you from?' the presenter asks Pol.

For a second, as we still don't really know Pol, we worry that he harbours some kind of resentment. That he will say he doesn't feel like a Peninsular, that his parents' families come from one of the ex-Colonies (an homage to his father's nostalgic narrative and to the memory of his mother), or that he will defend the indigenous people from the part of the Peninsula where he was born and raised (a reflex that comes from what he learnt at school as a little boy). But Pol stares into the camera as if he were incapable of understanding what's happening. He looks absent, afraid, as if he were suffering an attack of paranoia – something like that, or a mixture of all of it. In the resulting pause, the older man cuts in (the camera pulls back to take him in), claps Pol affection-ately on the shoulder a couple of times and says the name of the city. Pol tries to smile, and the presenter wraps up this section of the programme.

13

'I saw you on TV,' Gastón writes to Pol on the instant messaging app on his phone. 'You looked really thin – are you all right?' he asks. He feels more comfortable resorting to the cliché of worried parent, emotionally blackmailing Pol for the supposed deterioration of his physical appearance (something it's possible to weigh up objectively, in case it's called into question), rather than openly expressing concern at the boy's psychological state, at how disturbed he looked on the screen. He can't tell him what he's thinking: that Pol looked anxious, frightened, bewildered, troubled, gripped by the same unease he has radiated in the last few video calls, now accentuated by his erratic behaviour on the programme.

Gastón checks that the app has sent his messages, then gets up to have a wash and get ready to go and see Max; it's evening now, and the city team is playing tonight. He washes his arms, face and armpits in the tiny sink he has installed in the tool shed, a vague sense of suspicion forming in his mind, a sense that something isn't quite right; he is still thinking about the programme, which didn't explain what the research team Pol is part of is really doing. Everything they spoke about was theoretical, although what they're doing in the Tundra does actually have a very practical, concrete application. Pol told Max and Gastón when he was selected, and he informed them, rather ceremoniously, that this was confidential information, that the project was secret; Gastón thought he was exaggerating to make himself seem important; he now discovers, however, that this might have been true, because nothing of this was mentioned in the TV programme.

The focus of the institute where Pol works is the development of a hot-water rotary drill to bore into the ice without contaminating it. This instrument is used to extract microorganisms from the Tundra's subglacial lakes, and Pol's work consists of taking measurements to test how sterile the process is. If they were to make a hole in the ice with a pick, Pol had said by way of example, without taking care to ensure that the pick remained sterile the whole time, the samples obtained would be useless. At some point in the future, a tool such as this will be sent into space to drill down into the surface of Jupiter and Saturn's frozen moons, and it's crucial for us to guarantee that, if a bacterium is found there, it doesn't turn out that we took it there ourselves. Even though it sounds fantastical, this is not science fiction; Gastón checked online after talking to Pol: there are several similar space exploration projects, and Pol's group is just one more in the race to see who can patent the best tool and walk away with a contract worth millions.

Gastón finishes sprucing himself up, grabs his jacket, because now that the sun has gone it's starting to feel cooler, puts on Kitten's lead and then checks his phone again. 'I'm going away for a few days, so you won't be able to reach me,' we see Pol write, ignoring Gastón's concerns. 'I tried to tell

Dad, but he won't answer my calls. I'll let you know when I'm back.' Fieldwork, Gastón imagines; they must be going to look for little creatures in the ice. 'OK,' he writes back, 'look after yourself.'

14

The city team has another game, this time in the continental championships. While it's on, Gastón inspects the fridges. He has brought all the plastic containers in from the kitchen so he can keep one eye on the giant screen. Anything he finds in a good state he puts into the freezer. Or in no worse than a dubious state, at least. Anything that's gone off he tips into a huge black bag made of heavy-duty plastic, which he found in the cleaning cupboard. Max lets him do it. He's not even watching the match: he's become addicted to the multicoloured sweety game.

'These things aren't going to sort themselves out,' Gastón says, in a pause between inspecting one fridge and another, as if he were speaking, in the abstract, about Max's life, even though really he's talking about concrete things. 'At this rate you won't be able to hand over the space in time.'

He tells Max that the new owners are North Easterners, that he ought to talk to them and ask for an extension, buy a few more days' time. Max doesn't even look up from his phone. He does not say anything, either. His stubbly cheeks and the T-shirt full of holes from a music festival held in the Far West in the nineties of the previous century give a pretty good idea of the state of his new hygiene and personal grooming routine.

'The least you could do,' Gastón says, 'is have a shower.'

So this stench of an ancient cupboard that's been sealed for years, of damp, of sour dust, is emanating from Max (we hadn't managed to confirm this until now).

'Come on pal, when did you last brush your teeth?' he insists. 'Your breath stinks worse than Kitten's.'

On the various screens, the best footballer on Earth runs diagonally from the edge of the pitch towards the middle, the ball at his feet, dodging the defenders from the Northern team. The sound is off again and this muffles the emotion slightly, downgrades it, but we have experienced this hundreds of times and can add the ambient noise ourselves: a murmur that grows gradually louder until it becomes a loud yelling, the prelude to a goal.

'We've got to put Kitten to sleep,' Gastón says, suddenly, out of nowhere. He is holding a plastic container full of chicken with mushrooms in his hands. The bad kind of mushroom, not the good kind. Mushrooms associated with decay, mycotoxins, poison. The funk emanating from the food makes him speed up the operation. He pours the contents into the black bag and stops to look at his friend. Two tears well up and roll down Max's cheeks.

Max cries, without any fanfare, with no dramatic gestures, a muffled, discreet weeping, accompanied by the sure-footed gallop of the best footballer on Earth, who continues to elude the legs of his opponents as the only proof that time has not stopped. Gastón looks at Max's tears and at the multicoloured gleam of the sweeties on the screen of his friend's phone. We wonder what kind of crying this is, what kind of hormones and chemical elements it is made of; whether Max is crying in order to flush out the sadness hormones, or whether this crying will in fact increase his sense of helplessness. And then the best footballer on Earth finally finds the space to shoot, kicks the ball with his left foot, and misses.

15

As he's leaving the restaurant, Gastón sees El Tucu cross the road and start walking towards him. The shutters are already halfway through their descent.

'Have you got five minutes?' El Tucu asks.

Did Max and El Tucu part on good terms? Gastón isn't sure and he would quite like to know, so that he can prepare, so that he knows what attitude he should adopt. He replies that he does.

'Buy me a beer,' El Tucu says.

They walk in silence along the streets leading to the bar where the restaurant staff used to meet after closing for the night, to have a drink together before heading home. They sit down at a table a way off from the bar; Kitten curls up at Gastón's feet; they order two beers.

In the restaurant's kitchen, El Tucu was always the joker, but he looks deadly serious now. He places one brown, chubby hand on top of the other on the table, self-importantly, like a priest who's the headmaster at a religious school.

'Max has checked out,' he says. 'There's a way to save the restaurant, and he doesn't want to fight. But you get it, right? I heard you want to buy the premises and become a partner in the business.'

Their beers arrive. Gastón uses the pause to regret agreeing to this meeting so easily; he curses himself silently, using one of Max's words over and over again. For some reason, whenever he wants to use an insult he always reaches for a word from Max's vocabulary, as if acknowledging its semantic or phonetic superiority.

'It was an idea,' Gastón replies, 'just an idea.'

'But you've got money,' El Tucu insists.

Gastón knows that he has every right to decline to confirm this interrogative statement, which is an attempt to impose a particular direction on the conversation.

'Let me tell you what we can do,' El Tucu says.

The use of the plural unsettles Gastón. Is El Tucu referring to an organised group? To the association the lawyer from the country told him about? Or does this plural include him before the fact, without his consent, like a threat?

'We squeeze the Far Easterners,' El Tucu explains, 'we use residents to create pressure, we intimidate them, make their lives impossible.'

'They're North Easterners,' Gastón corrects him.

'Whatever!' El Tucu replies. 'There are a couple of local councillors backing us. We do a big social media push, we'll get TV people to come, the press – we'll force them to sell.'

'I'm not going to buy it,' Gastón says. 'I'm not interested anymore.'

El Tucu uncrosses his hands on the table. Neither man has touched his beer. El Tucu looks at Gastón contemptuously, as if trying to intimidate him. Only now do we realise something: if Tucu used to tell jokes, it wasn't to cheer people up, but rather a method of control; he would dictate what was said and how, who was laughed at and how. El Tucu, for instance, is one of those who says that the best footballer on Earth isn't really the best, that he's soft, a spoilt little boy who needed growth hormones and is out of his depth. He is one of those who would rather be on the other team, running after him, trying to get the ball off him, with a dirty tackle if necessary.

'Five of us are out on our arses now,' El Tucu says, after downing half his beer in one go, 'plus the two or three from the high season. These people don't hire anyone; they keep it all very cosy among themselves. We've got kids, families. If only we were as lucky as you, if only we knew as much about geography.'

Gastón avoids El Tucu's reproachful gaze, his accusations, that age-old resentment which is the driving force behind revolutions and raids. He raises his right arm and scribbles something in the air to ask for the bill. He tries to concentrate on something else, but he can hear El Tucu's heavy breathing, his telepathic insults. He won't look at him again. He will pay for the beers and get out of there without saying a word. He will hurry forwards, towards the future, towards the next few pages, he is wishing with all his might that the full-stop-new-paragraph that will take us to the next chapter would appear. On the next table he notices the sports section of today's paper, the headline that announces that the best footballer on Earth's participation in the next game is in doubt, that his nausea and vomiting episodes have not let up.

16

Gastón still hasn't had a reply from the Association of Traditional Healers, and the email address he finds online returns his messages because it was deactivated a long time ago. The association has no office, no opening hours for either members or customers, no physical address, no kind of infrastructure at all.

He does, however, get two or three phone calls a day from the veterinary clinic. One in the morning, a couple more in the afternoon. He never answers them. One message a day, as night falls: 'Please get in touch as a matter of urgency to arrange a time for us to carry out the procedure.'

Gastón decides to wait. He hasn't given up his hope of finding a sedatoress.

17

When he wakes up, his phone has lots of messages, hundreds, because of the time difference with the Southern Cone. What's the point of him being ahead in time, if the past is just waiting for him to open his eyes? He's been added to a group one of his cousins created; they're making plans to celebrate the anniversary of the death of his grandfather, the family patriarch. Gastón moves his finger across the phone's screen to get to the first few messages and read the details of the party, which will be next month, in the function room of a social club in the city where he was born and lived until he was twenty-six years old. There are cousins planning on travelling from the capital city and a few who, like Gastón, live far away, although they live to the north of the Southern Cone, in the Northern Cone, at the far limits of the West.

After discussing logistics, and who has confirmed and who hasn't, the family starts using the group to find out what everyone's up to. There are photos of nephews and nieces Gastón didn't even know existed, of cousins he struggles to recognise, because he stopped hanging out with them when he was a teenager or, at the very latest, before he made the move over to the Peninsula; announcements of the death of distant aunts and uncles, of weddings, divorces, pregnancies, new businesses, and an invitation to all those who live abroad to visit the hair salon belonging to one of his cousins when they come over, where they can also get a manicure and pedicure done.

Twice, people ask about Gastón (we can't tell who, as Gastón doesn't have their numbers stored in his phone). Where is he? What's he up to these days? Someone says that he's still in the Peninsula, a few others speculate that he never returned since he left, thirty years ago, maybe more, after his father died. Someone else says that they all know what Gastón was like: a little bit odd, even as a child. That he chose to sell off his father's businesses for a song, that he was never interested in business and so was scammed, given any old price because all he wanted to do was take the money and run away. Other people say that he wouldn't have needed the businesses anyway, what with all the properties he inherited. At that point the group admin (who we imagine must have not been following the conversation for the last few minutes) warns them that Gastón is reading all this, that he got his phone number from the estate agent that deals with the properties his father left him, that one of the agents is his brother-in-law. A few people say hi to Gastón, ask him how he is, what he's up to these days, whether he's got a family, if perhaps he has spawned a little coloniser; they tell him he should use the party as an excuse to visit the city, say they miss him.

He finishes reading the messages, still in bed, stretching, and then scrolls through the app's settings; he blocks a few of the group's members (four or five – not that many, if we consider that there are more than twenty of them); and then leaves the group without writing anything and deletes it completely.

18

Another message on Gastón's phone. It's the lawyer from the country. He says they're organising a local barbecue to grill elongated onions and raise funds for the neighbourhood's traditional tradespeople. That they've decided Gastón's little market garden would be the ideal spot for it, and they could even buy the elongated onions from him, so that only elongated onions grown in local earth are consumed, but that he would expect Gastón to contribute by donating the produce. He then suggests a couple of dates, two Sundays within the next two or three weeks, and asks Gastón to choose whichever is the most convenient.

He's so obsessed with the earth, Gastón exclaims, out loud, to himself, so we can hear him. Elongated onions aren't even from around here – they were brought from somewhere not far away to the south-west, and in any case, elongated onion barbecues are a winter tradition, not early spring. Gastón has actually grown them late this year at the request of one of his customers, who serves them deep-fried as part of the set menu at his restaurant, a fusion of food from the Southern Cone and Far Eastern cuisine, brought together using the technique of tempura, which came over from the Far East to the ex-Colonies in the Far West two centuries ago.

Gastón lets the instant messaging app notify the lawyer from the country that he has read his message, and doesn't reply.

19

The administrative advisor is speaking on the phone; she makes a gesture that is an attempt to wave hello and goodbye at the same time, apologising for being busy, and bends down briefly to stroke Kitten's head. She is about to keep walking to wherever it is that she's going, but Gastón steps in front of her, takes her by the arm and lets her know with hand signals that he needs to speak to her. We hear her try to arrange a date with the person on the other end of the phone, something to do with a meeting in a bank, enunciating the native language with that over-the-top diction that is the hallmark of those who have never left the city and are proud of this fact.

They press up close against the wall so as not to obstruct the narrow pavement completely, and when Kitten realises that they are waiting he flops down onto the flowery tiles. Gastón averts his eyes, so that the interruption isn't interpreted as an invasion of privacy on top of everything else, but we take advantage of the fact that the administrative advisor can't see us to take her in slowly from head to toe: her heels, her ivory suit and subtle make-up, not so vulgar that it stands out, nor so modest that it goes unnoticed, appropriate for someone who has to deal with clients face to face. That pale skin. Those blue eyes.

'Coffee?' Gastón asks her when, at last, she ends the call.

'He told me he'd go back,' she replies.

'What?' Gastón says.

'He told me he'd go back to his homeland,' the administrative advisor says.

The unexpected turn the conversation is taking disarms Gastón. He can't tell if this was the strategy Max used to fob her off, or if he really is thinking of leaving and hasn't told him yet.

'Why don't you come by the restaurant?' Gastón says. 'I reckon that would cheer him up.'

'I'm sick of this,' replies the administrative advisor, 'it's so annoying. Why isn't he straight with me? Why does he have to lie?'

Gastón apologises for Max, says his friend is all mixed up, that all this trouble with the restaurant has been hard and it's paralysed him; it's not that he's reacted badly, it's that he hasn't reacted at all.

'He made me find Ona a job at the administrative agency,' she says, following the logic suggested by the flow of her thoughts rather than that of the conversation. 'He asked me to give her a break, and then Pol left and as far as I know they're not even together anymore, and now I'm stuck with Ona – the poor girl's a bit slow but I feel bad, I can't fire her.'

It's pointless to push it, Gastón realises; the relationship was a short one, a few months at most, like all of Max's relationships, but long enough for the administrative advisor to accumulate an undeniable list of grievances. He tugs on Kitten's lead to make the dog get up.

'I shouldn't have bothered you,' he says.

'Listen,' the administrative advisor says.

Gastón pauses in his attempted goodbye and we see the advisor hesitate, carefully choosing the words of whatever it is she is about to say.

'I know you want to help Max,' she says, 'but you've got to be careful. It's a bad idea for people to associate you with certain people, for them to think you're on one side or the other. Things are really strange right now.'

'With certain people?' Gastón repeats, but inflecting it like a question.

If the administrative advisor really likes people to be straight with her, Gastón thinks, then she can piss right off with this faux-confused rhetorical formulation, a cowardly euphemism.

'You know perfectly well what I'm talking about,' she says.

20

On the radio he hears that the endocrinologist who works for the city team has ruled out the vomiting being a side effect of the growth hormones, and says that this theory doesn't make sense, because it's been thirteen years since the best footballer on Earth was last prescribed them. Gastón is earthing up the elongated onions so they don't become bulbous. One day, in the not-too-distant future, he will have to resign himself to hiring a labourer to help him with this sort of task. Kneeling down and heaping the earth up around each of the bulbs not only lengthens the stalk on the alliums, it also makes the muscles in his shoulder blades spasm. He has one earphone in his left ear, and the other ear is free so that he can hear Kitten, who has stretched out on the little makeshift bed Gastón has laid down for him in the shade of the tool shed's veranda. The voices on the radio, inside his head, muffle his own, mute it, try to cancel it out. We listen, too.

There is speculation that the best footballer on Earth suffers from nausea before games, which might be caused by digestive or psychological problems – gastritis, stress, anxiety attacks. The presenters speak to a gastroenterologist on the phone, and he lists foods that cause acid reflux. Tomato-based sauces, chocolate, red wine, fizzy drinks, peppers, citrus fruits, processed flour. The mention of bread leads to a lengthy discussion (which the gastroenterologist does not take part in) about the possibility that the best footballer on Earth has a gluten intolerance. Until a coeliac phones in from the archipelago located an hour ahead to the West to inform listeners that what he felt before being diagnosed, before modifying his diet, was that his belly was swollen and tight, as if it were going to explode and splatter his guts all over the walls and ceiling. Then it's back to psychology. Is the best footballer on Earth suffering from anxiety attacks? The listeners vote online. Then a news report is read out from the best footballer on Earth's native land: the ex-manager of the national team has aired his opinion on a TV programme about the footballer's health, making rather pessimistic predictions about the man's ability to win the World Cup for his team. 'It's useless trying to make a leader out of a man who goes to the toilet twenty times before a game,' he declares. Out loud, to the ex-manager, Gastón directs the string of mother-related insults from Max's vocabulary, the one that we, too, out of sheer repetition, are growing accustomed to.

The heated debate unleashed by what the manager has said is interrupted by a call from another listener, who says that he knows the truth about what's going on. He says this so emphatically that he causes quite a stir. He says that the best footballer on Earth is an extraterrestrial, a reptile with digestive problems that come from eating a terrestrial diet. The presenters burst out laughing.

Gastón has finished earthing up the bulbs in this particular plot. He takes off his gardening gloves and sits back on his heels. He goes to the radio app on his phone to pause it, and before doing so catches the conspiracy-theorist listener saying that reptiles and arthropods come from planets where evolution developed differently to how it did on Earth, and that the Greys, meanwhile, are humanoids and are something like our distant cousins.

21

Inside the restaurant, he presses the button that lowers the shutters and then hears Max's irritated voice yelling from the dining area.

'I told you it was Gastón. Come out of there; don't be ridiculous.'

Max's father slowly appears behind the bar as he gets to his feet. When was the last time he was here? Gastón wonders; it was around seven or eight years ago, he reckons. That might be a long time or not; time doesn't move in the same way for everyone. By this point it has turned Max's father into a leathery old piece of parchment. A swollen piece of parchment, to be precise, what with that balloon-like belly of his. The life of a criminal, Gastón thinks; or rather, a criminally good life: too much sugar, too much sitting around, too much sun, all sorts of happiness hormones and sleeping pills.

Max's father strides out from behind the bar and gives Gastón's arm such a powerful squeeze that he manages to upset Kitten. The dog goes on the alert to defend his master.

'Easy,' Gastón says; 'it's Pol's grandfather, don't you remember?'

His agreeable tone convinces Kitten, who walks over to his favourite spot by the bar and flops down between two stools.

'No one can know I'm here,' Max's father says.

'You've seen way too many films,' Gastón replies.

'I'm not in the mood for jokes,' Max's father retorts.

'I know,' Gastón says, 'you're the most wanted man from your town.'

Max stays sitting at one of the tables in the dining area, his head bent over his phone, devoted to his reverie of multicoloured sweeties. The grotesque contrast between Max's father's exaggerated resolve and his son's recent apathy reminds Gastón that these visits tend to end abruptly. He himself once had to intervene to help Max's father change his flight home to an earlier one. But this is different. This time there will be no power struggle, that constant battle to impose a certain way of doing things, to judge the other man's decisions, to attribute blame and to feel victimised. This time, Max's father will have no adversary.

'Could you not think of a worse hiding place?' Gastón continues. 'It's no secret Max lives here, or that you've got a passport from this part of the world.'

'I didn't use that passport,' Max's father says.

'You've got another one?

'The one from my fourth wife, the good passport. It cost me an arm and a leg.'

Max's father puts his right hand into his trouser pocket and extracts the document with its blue cover from the other ex-Colonies, the prosperous ones, the ones that the Islanders from the North snatched from the Peninsulars centuries ago. Has Max's father spawned another descendant in the interval since his last visit?

'What's wrong with this guy?' Max's father asks, jerking his head towards the table where his son is sitting.

Gastón takes his time to reflect properly on how he is going to respond; he wants to help his friend, but loyalty comes first. He weighs up one explanation, then another. Perhaps Max's father's visit might drag Max kicking and screaming into the land of the living. Ultimately, he was the one who gave Max the money to open the restaurant and who kept him afloat until eventually it was in the black. You could say that with this money he had cleared a debt, with Max and Max's mother, but Gastón knows Max's father will see it as his son having squandered his inheritance.

'Shall we put the game on?' Gastón says. 'It's about to start.'

He walks to the dining area to look for the control that turns on the audiovisual system. As he gets closer to Max, his friend motions to him to sit down next to him; based on what we can smell, it looks like – it smells like – Max has tipped an entire bottle of cologne over himself, as if in deference to his father's arrival, or rather, to prevent his father from forcing him to have a shower, from treating him like a child. The strange cocktail, however, does not work; the resulting aroma is unpleasant and, as if that weren't enough, unnerving. Where has Max been, what has he been doing? it would make anyone ask, which would force him to give more sophisticated answers than his usual excuse of a simple lack of hygiene.

It is a smell, then, that distracts, as it has distracted us, and we almost miss Max secretly showing his phone to Gastón, motioning at him to keep quiet. He doesn't want his father to see what he's doing. For a moment we envision him bragging about his world-beating score in the multicoloured sweetie game.

They are messages from Pol's boss, asking if Max's son has come home. He hasn't shown up at the lab for days, hasn't slept in his dorm room, and no one has seen him or knows anything. He explains that this may not be a reason to be alarmed, that it's normal for some researchers not to be able to bear the inhuman conditions of the Tundra, that runaways are relatively common. Most of them come back, he says, and the university simply ramps up the level of psychological support they are offered.

There are several messages, from two, three days ago. When he scrolls down with his finger on the screen of the phone, to make time pass, the questions increase in intensity, in urgency; despairingly, Pol's boss says that he is responsible for reporting back to the investors.

Max has not replied.

22

When at long last the president of the Association of Traditional Healers gets back to him, he turns out to be more interested in promoting his own services, or those of the members from whom he receives a commission, we imagine, than in listening to what Gastón is asking. He says that he is a canine shaman – a certified one. That meditation has been shown to be effective in terminal illnesses in all kinds of pets, including rabbits and canaries. Gastón insists on the sedatoress and, in return, is offered two sessions of electromagnetic therapy for the price of one.

'I can see I've made a mistake,' Gastón says, irritably. 'Thanks anyway.'

'Wait,' the president of the association quickly replies.

The silence at the other end of the line gives us hope that the president of the association might be consulting the list of members, if such a thing exists, although it's more likely that what he is actually doing is consulting his memory.

'I need to have a look through our records,' he says, which confirms to us that, just as we feared, this list does not exist. 'I'll call you in a couple of days.'

'It's urgent,' Gastón replies; 'the dog needs palliative care now.'

'Nothing is urgent,' the president of the association says; 'all pain is a reflection of the past, and can melt away in the present; I can demonstrate it if you let me hypnotise the dog.'

'I look forward to your call,' Gastón says, and hangs up.

23

The two men intercept Gastón as he's leaving the supermarket, before he starts heading back up the hill that takes him home. They introduce themselves, saying that they are from the same place as him, as if to make it clear that they know where Gastón comes from, despite the fact that, strictly speaking, they are not even from the same place as one another, because one says he is from the Cordillera and the other from the Pacific Coast. Their inflection, their vocabulary, the way their hair is styled, their gestures – everything points to a recent relocation here, not more than five years ago. 'We're from the association of traders,' says the guy from the Pacific Coast. 'I own the corner shop by the main avenue.'

'I run the internet café here,' Cordillera Guy says, and Gastón realises they've stopped him right outside an internet café.

They want to know if he has a big fridge out at the market garden, to chill the beers for the barbecue. Gastón tells them that he doesn't know what they're talking about. Pacific Coast Guy reminds him of the lawyer from the country's visit, the barbecue of elongated onions to raise money. Gastón insists that he doesn't understand.

'See that there?' Cordillera Guy asks, pointing with out-stretched arm at a shop being refitted on the next street. 'Remember what it was before? A farm shop. That's where the old folk used to go and buy their little daily ration of milk, their cheese, their eggs, their butter. Guess who it belongs to now? Guess what they're going to open?'

Gastón tells them he knows the owner of this shop and that he's decided to retire; he found a client who paid him what he was asking for the change of ownership – maybe a little less, but that was normal in any business deal.

'They retired him, mate,' Pacific Coast Guy says. 'His sons were going to take over the business – that would have been the normal thing.'

The sons are both engineers and work for transterritorial companies, Gastón recalls, but before saying anything he also remembers that it's futile trying to reason with people who use shared origin as a way of striking up a conversation or as an argument, and so he opts to keep quiet instead. Cordillera Guy comes up very close, brushing up against him, invading his space.

'You can't be on two sides,' he says.

'I'm not on any side,' Gastón replies.

'You can't not be on any side,' Cordillera Guy insists.

Gastón says that he didn't know they were at war. Pacific Coast Guy grows exasperated. It's clear that he finds civilised intimidation restrictive, like a T-shirt several sizes too small.

'What planet do you live on, mate?' he asks.

What planet do you live on, Gastón repeats to himself, and there is so much violence, so much desire for exclusion in this question, that it seems like a threat of eviction; there's no room for you here – go and live on another planet. Gastón pulls on Kitten's lead, steps around Cordillera Guy and walks off.

24

He stretches out his arm and gropes around on the bedside table for his phone. The alarm is going to go off in two minutes, and in any case, he can tell he will have notifications from messages he's received while he slept. Quickly he unlocks the screen, Pol and Max on his mind; maybe Pol has finally turned up. We see how the light illuminates Gastón's bleary-eyed face, how he blinks to protect his eyeballs from the artificial assault. Kitten whimpers a little yawn and stretches his legs from his spot on his makeshift bed.

'Morning, buddy,' Gastón says, fumbling with his phone to get to the instant messaging app.

But it isn't news of Pol. Once again the time difference, the messages from the past, from the Southern Cone. It's a cousin he's never had a relationship with – this we ascertain not only because the number is not in his contacts, or because we hear Gastón wonder out loud who it can be, but because he spends the first few messages introducing himself, explaining how they're related; he is the eldest son of one of Gastón's cousins, Gastón's father's older sister's son's son. He tells him that his father, Gastón's cousin, doesn't know that he's going to write to him; he corrects himself, that he is writing to him (that he wrote to him, we correct him);

but that he and his siblings have decided to look for Gastón because they've spoken to a lawyer and, although their father doesn't agree (the father of this cousin, Gastón's cousin), the lawyer has told them that they have the right to claim part of their great-grandfather's inheritance (the inheritance left by Gastón's grandfather, by Gastón's father's father), because he (the great-grandfather) did not act proportionally when he left all those properties to Gastón's father, and it isn't fair that he, Gastón, is the only one who has benefitted and continues to benefit from this inheritance. That, although it is true that their great-grandfather left a lot of money to their grandmother (Gastón's father's sister), the amount, what with the time that has passed, is completely disproportionate, because this money became gradually devalued with each economic crisis, and since their grandmother didn't know how to handle finances and, furthermore, was given bad advice, what she left to her children, among them his father (Gastón's cousin), is not comparable to the inheritance Gastón received.

Gastón studies, without reading them, the messages that follow: several more long, wordy messages, composed with unorthodox spelling and fractured syntax; he swipes his finger down to make the app notify the sender that he's read them, then goes to the settings, blocks the nephew and deletes the conversation, which, if we're being precise, was really a monologue.

25

'You'll need to say that you're calling on my behalf,' the president of the Association of Traditional Healers says, after giving him the sedatoress's phone number.

Gastón hangs up and, as he dials the number the man has given him, muses with a smile on how it turns out that pyramids really are powerful, but more as a marketing strategy for supernatural products. The sedatoress doesn't answer the phone, but a few minutes later she sends him a message via the instant messaging app asking him what he needs. Perhaps in order to quash one of the likely turns the conversation will take, to ensure that it doesn't tip over into the magical or the miraculous (so the sedatoress understands that he doesn't believe in the occult, so as not to ruin this story), Gastón takes care to type out his messages with the greatest objectivity he can muster.

He explains that he has a dog who is ill, terminally ill and in pain, and that he wants to provide him with palliative care and then have him put to sleep; it has to be at home, he writes, at the market garden he has, rather, and he doesn't want to take the dog anywhere else, and so she would need to come to where the two of them are. The sedatoress replies equally coolly: she lets him know the price of the service, asks for the address and informs him that she will be there the following day, towards the evening.

Once they have finished exchanging messages, Gastón looks at the photograph the sedatoress has as her profile picture on the app, looks at her eyes, those slanted eyes that might signal her background like a finger on a map, that make us stop looking at the sedatoress and instead to infer the group, the Far Easterners, their food, their budget bazaars, their languages, their spirituality, their silences, everything that makes up our incomprehension.

26

Gastón hears the whistles and Kitten's ears go up as if his whole body were getting up, as if he were running over to the entrance to the market garden, but pain stops him from doing either of these things, and so he makes do with smiling. The smile of a dog lying down, ill, a smile not with his muzzle but with his tail, which he thumps happily on the ground, making the sound of a broom as it sweeps the floor of the tool shed.

'I told you he was OK,' Gastón tells Kitten, relieved, out loud, although really he says it to himself and to let us know who it is that's arrived.

He puts down the gloves he was looking for and walks back up the path leading to the gate. Pol is waiting for him on the other side, his hands in the pockets of a jacket that is too warm for the almost-out-of-winter temperature.

'You lock this now?' Pol asks, accustomed to the gate to Gastón's market garden always being open.

'It's so the tourists can't get in,' Gastón lies, unbolting the gate and removing the padlock.

'Has something happened?' Pol says.

'I got tired of them just wandering in to ask if the place is a historic monument, like the park,' Gastón replies.

They throw their arms around each other. Gastón notes, as he squeezes Pol's body with the effusiveness of genuine affection, that the boy is shivering. He also notes that he has got thinner.

'Where's Kitten?' Pol asks.

'He's down there.'

'He's not going to come up?'

'He's been chasing mice,' Gastón lies again; 'you know what he's like.'

They are lies whose useful life will be very short, minutes at most, and Gastón knows it. He needs to tell Pol everything that has happened, but he wants to preserve this moment of innocence, receive the boy's spontaneous hug, before the bad news. They walk down the little slope, commenting on the weather. Pol says that he's really cold, that he's been knocked off balance by the abrupt change in temperature.

'When did you arrive?' Gastón asks.

He realises that Pol is weighing up whether to tell him the truth or to carry on, just as Gastón is, with the white lies.

'Three days ago,' he says, a little falteringly.

'And where have you been?' Gastón asks.

'At my girlfriend's house,' he replies; 'my ex, I mean,' he corrects himself.

'You were with Mariona?'

Pol nods. Before Gastón can ask him to explain, he adds, quickly, 'I wasn't ready to see you both,' he says, 'you, Dad; I needed some time.'

As they walk over to the tool shed they can make out the outline of Kitten's body, lying on his little makeshift bed.

'Have you seen your dad yet?' Gastón asks. 'We were worried.'

'What's up with Kitten?' Pol asks.

'Do you know your grandfather's here?' Gastón replies.

'What's going on?' Pol says.

'What do you mean?' Gastón replies. 'Nothing.'

'Nothing?' Pol says. 'What does that message on the wall outside mean?'

27

Two bits of graffiti on the wall surrounding the market garden. One visible to the tourists in the Historic Park, the other so big that it can be seen from the main road. Written in capital letters, in red paint and in the same scrawl as the other messages that have been appearing in the neighbourhood, such as *Incomers Out* or *No More Incomers*.

TRAITOR

28

He hesitates again, just before going into the bazaar, but does go in; he has to tug hard on Kitten's lead, practically dragging him, because the dog seems to have a memory of the pain he felt on this part of the street. Gastón's qualms turn out to have been for nothing, because behind the counter stands not Yu, but his wife. He wishes her a good day and explains that he needs some spray paint.

It's early, the shop is empty, and so the woman comes with him. At around noon the retirees looking to replace a kitchen utensil or buy some cleaning product or other will arrive, and in the afternoon the children, who will try to wheedle a fancy dress costume, some batteries, a notebook or a football out of their grandparents. The monotony of the neighbourhood, the final nail in the coffin provided by the tourists visiting the Historic Park, who purchase whatever they forget to bring from home, or didn't foresee they'd need: a towel, a hat to protect them from the sun.

Amidst the array of colours, Gastón notices a row of cans of invisible paint. The ingenuity of the Far Easterners makes him smile – they are excellent businesspeople, no doubt about it. He picks up one of the containers, out of curiosity, to read the label.

'That's the one we sell the most of,' the woman says; 'twenty or thirty cans a week.'

Gastón doesn't know if this is a lot or hardly any; it seems like a lot to him if this is a joke product, and very little if it really does work. The weight of the can in his hand tells him it does contain some sort of liquid.

'It's only visible in UV light,' the woman explains.

'Really?' he asks.

'Oh yes,' the woman replies, 'come and see.'

Before following her, Gastón selects two cans of black paint; the woman picks up a little torch on her way out to the street.

'Here,' she says to Gastón.

She points to the wall at the side of the shop, adjacent to the large front window, where we can't see anything. She turns on the torch and, as she moves the UV light closer to the wall, we start to see an M, an O, a G, a W, an A and an I appear. Gastón looks at the woman, waiting for her to explain the meaning of the word.

'It's one of our words,' she says, 'a bad word. There are bad people round here, people who don't like us.'

The Far Easterners are selling the same invisible paint that's used to insult them, and in secret, no less? Gastón doesn't understand a thing, or perhaps he half understands it, understands it badly, as we do. He would like to ask the woman to explain, but he fears he might make another gaffe (might suggest, without meaning to, that the Far Easterners' instinct for business is stronger than their survival instinct). He is saved from making a faux pas by Yu, who at that moment rounds the corner with his two children. He sees Gastón, the torch in his wife's hand, and says something in one of the many languages spoken in the Far East; tells his family to get inside the shop, we figure, because this is what the woman does, followed by the two children.

'That's the product that gets stolen the most from the shop,' Yu says. 'Five or ten cans a week.'

Now we understand even less, but the Far Easterner is about to say something else, and so we'd better be quiet and pay attention, and perhaps we'll be able to draw some sort of conclusion.

'It's a sign,' Yu says. 'They're marking us out.'

He takes out a cigarette, lights it and starts to smoke, staring at the wall where, without the torch, we can't see the message. Intrigued, people walking past on the pavement also stare at the wall, mirroring him, trying to make out what's so interesting about this blank space to make Gastón and the Far Easterner stare so hard at it.

'They're plotting something,' the Far Easterner says.

He smokes intently, as if he were a detective examining the scene of a crime; the evidence that leads to the culprits must be around here somewhere, on the wall and on the pavement (fingerprints, shoe prints, traces of deoxyribonucleic acid), although the real explanation will have to be sought beyond this street or this neighbourhood (insecurity, economic crisis, a distorted territorialism, fear hormones).

'Why don't you take the stock off the shelves?' Gastón ventures.

He seems to be saying that dead dogs don't bite, but the cans of invisible paint are not the dog, and the messages are not the biting (the dog is the fear hormones, and the biting is hatred). We don't know if Yu knows this saying, or if there is an equivalent in the collection of Far Eastern proverbs; what we do know is that Gastón is the least qualified person there is to talk about dead dogs.

The Far Easterner says that the cans of invisible paint are a good product for them, that graffiti artists buy them to sign the works they create on walls.

'And in any case,' he adds, 'I've just installed a camera in the alleyway; I'm going to catch them red-handed. It's the only way to find out what they're up to.'

We don't quite manage to determine what it is that Gastón finds more touching: Yu's struggle with the letter R after choosing the word 'red-handed', or the excitement with which he explains his detective-novel-like plans.

29

Mogwai means 'evil spirit' in one of the many languages spoken in the Far East; but chiefly, and Gastón remembers this now, as he reads the results of the search on his phone's browser, it is the name of some fantastic Far Eastern creatures in a film from the twentieth century. This isn't a coincidence; if we do the maths, we will see that it was a commercial success in the period when the protagonists of this story were young.

In the film, a failed inventor, a family man, is looking for a present for his son and buys an adorable little creature, a kind of living soft toy, in a Far Eastern bazaar. The creature comes with a strict list of instructions for its care, including a set of rules that must not be disobeyed (it mustn't be fed after midnight, it mustn't come into contact with water). The son is careless, and the adorable creature multiplies, but in its evil incarnation: a murderous little monster that destroys the city.

Gastón recalls the endless references made in the film to the poor quality of Far Eastern products, especially electronic devices. In the midst of all the explosions and bloody killings, it was hard to spot that this was in fact protectionist propaganda from the other ex-Colonies in the Far West, the prosperous ones, the ones that the Islanders from the North snatched from the Peninsulars centuries ago.

30

Standing at the entrance to the market garden, the sedatoress tells him that the entire ceremony will take a week, and that, on the seventh day, the treatment should be performed in the same place as where the dog will be buried. Her role, she explains, is something like that of a celebrant. The choice of the joyful-sounding word 'celebrant' is as unfortunate as the phrase 'to carry out the procedure', but something must have got lost in translation; let's assume that the sedatoress doesn't have enough of a grasp of the colonising language to pick up on the lugubrious irony this word contains. This is how she introduced herself when she arrived, saying that she is the sedatoress, no name or surname, and Gastón hasn't asked her for these details, either, having convinced himself that there's a risk that a misunderstanding might ruin the performance.

'Where shall we do it?' the sedatoress asks.

Her gaze moves around the garden and stops at the carob tree's sturdy silhouette.

'We'll do it there,' she says, lifting her right hand to point with her index finger over at the tree. 'Is the market garden yours?'

Gastón nods, glumly, in spite of the fact that he knows it's the perfect spot. He's distracted, looking at the spider vein on the sedatoress's right cheek. The incredibly fine red lines, quivering like a cellar spider's long legs on her smooth skin. How old is she, the sedatoress? Probably around forty, Gastón guesses, as his eyes continue to run over those lines. The sedatoress senses his gaze but she is not embarrassed and does not tick him off; she must be used to it. There is something hypnotic about that spider, something that exerts a kind of macabre pull, as if reinforcing the sedatoress's supernatural aura, though her attire rather gives the lie to this (she is wearing a plain T-shirt, hiking trousers bristling with pockets, and a pair of what look like construction workers' boots).

They walk slowly down the slope to the carob, respecting the dog's unhurried pace. They settle down in the shade of the tree. The sedatoress explains to Gastón that she needs Kitten to stay lying down, that she hopes it won't be necessary to use any force; the animal needs to be on the ground even if they have to hold him down, she says, contradicting herself. The dog lies down on his own – this is the position he now spends most of the time in, to get away from the pain, and Gastón crouches down to be near him. The sedatoress says something in a Far Eastern language, perhaps in the same language as Yu, perhaps in another, something that sounds like 'good', or 'nice', like something you would say to a dog to praise it for good behaviour.

'What are you going to give him?' Gastón asks.

The sedatoress says it's a natural painkiller, tells him not to worry, it doesn't hurt, and that if it doesn't work it won't have any unwanted side effects. Gastón watches her open the little doctor's bag that stirred up so many misgivings when he greeted her at the gate. Bags like this usually hold terrible secrets, instruments of torture; needles and surgical tape, in this case. As the sedatoress moves her hands over the implements, Gastón repeats to himself that everything is going to be OK, everything is going to be OK, but he doesn't actually say anything, just looks into Kitten's eyes, as if this way his voice will leave his head and enter the dog's.

Suddenly, the sedatoress shouts out an insult, breaking off halfway through when she realises it's ruining the mysticism of the moment. She has pricked herself with one of the needles. She shouted the insult in the native language. Gastón thinks that she pronounced it with an accent from the outskirts of the city.

31

He says that he is only going to tell this story once. He doesn't want to repeat it, and so they all have to be together. Before settling down, Gastón takes the plates through to the kitchen and drags another table over to where Max, his father and Pol have just eaten, so that the four of them can be more comfortable. Apparently, Max is subsisting on a diet of defrosted food from the containers Gastón took the precaution of salvaging. Today, to celebrate the fact that the family has been reunited, they have chosen turkey in a sauce of peppers, chocolate, almonds and sesame seeds.

Pol asks Max to turn off his phone, saying that he won't tell them a thing unless his father puts the game away. He goes further: he asks everyone to switch off their phones; he doesn't trust these devices that are programmed to spy on you. Gastón laughs a little at Pol's lack of guile, at his naivety, but the boy will not continue until everyone obeys him.

Pol's grandfather is the most impatient, shifting restlessly in his seat to make it clear that all this mystery seems childish to him, as if they were forcing him to play hide-and-seek – him, a fugitive from justice! At least Max seems curious, interested. Can it be that what Pol is going to tell them is something capable of bringing him back down to Earth? If Pol is in some kind of trouble then this might end up awakening Max's dulled parental instincts. An obstacle to overcome might give new meaning to his existence, force him to act, to break out of this void. Max's void: the restaurant shutters down, the TVs all on, the microwave defrosting food, the multicoloured sweeties.

Pol clears his throat.

'We are not alone,' he says.

Pol's grandfather gives a start, glances towards the main room, inspecting the door to the restaurant.

'What do you mean?' he asks.

'There is life on other planets,' Pol says.

He stops speaking, to give the others time to process the news. Gastón and Max exchange glances, re-establishing for a moment their complicity and trying to work out whether Pol might be talking about a scientific discovery, or whether he might be suffering from an attack of paranoia. Pol's grandfather sees things in more black-and-white terms.

'I told you your brain was going to freeze,' he says.

'All the work we do in the Tundra is a smokescreen,' Pol explains. 'That's why I ran away. I discovered it by chance. I'm not supposed to know.'

32

The rhythm of Kitten's breathing gradually slows down; Gastón watches him give in to sleep, his hands telling him, resting as they are gently on the animal's head and back, that Kitten's body is surrendering. If a dog were capable of attaining spiritual peace, Gastón thinks, if a dog needed to believe that something called spiritual peace existed, we think along with Gastón, then it would look something like this. Kitten smiles, a smile made of slackened muscles and relaxed ears. His four legs are bent in perfect symmetry: the dog is all curled up. It is a moment of such absolute calm that we can hear how the elongated onions in the neighbouring plot are burrowing deeper into the earth, making a rustling sound as they bore down into it their process of elongation.

The sedatoress asks if he wants her to tell him Kitten's dreams, or if he would rather they sit in silence. Gastón is afraid to shatter this perfect calm; what's more, it troubles him that quackery might rear its ugly head at this precise moment, just as he has convinced himself that he was right to bring in the sedatoress, to choose her over the veterinary clinic. His first impulse, then, is to reply that no, he prefers quietness, this subdued sort of reality. But the sedatoress seems quite eager, as if narrating Kitten's dreams formed part of the ceremony she is performing and in which we do not fully trust. Gastón looks again at the spider vein on her right cheek. More than a spider, it now makes him think of a spiderweb. His gaze is caught there. The sedatoress begins to narrate a dream, and Gastón listens to her.

When she's finished, they are both laughing, in absolute fits; the sedatoress barely managed to finish her own story, she was spluttering so much.

'How do you think up so many ridiculous things?' Gastón asks her.

'I don't know,' she replies. 'I make it up. Does it bother you?'

Gastón shakes his head, still laughing.

'What did you give him?' he asks, nodding at Kitten.

'A little bit of morphine,' the sedatoress replies.

'Thank you,' Gastón says.

The sedatoress lets out a sigh, trying to get over the fit of giggles once and for all. She looks up at the carob tree's highest branches; then her gaze moves down and all around the outline of its protective shadow.

'It's nice here,' she says.

Gastón nods.

'What's your name?' he asks her.

The sedatoress utters her name, a traditional name for those indigenous to this part of the Peninsula.

'Seriously?' Gastón replies.

'Why, what is it?' the sedatoress says.

'Nothing,' Gastón replies. 'Fancy a beer?'

'I do – and some olives,' replies the sedatoress.

'I've got a bag of crisps,' Gastón says.

'That'll do,' the sedatoress says.

Gastón gets up to go to the tool shed, where he has a little fridge. When he comes back, he holds the can of beer out to the sedatoress.

'Listen,' says the sedatoress, carefully, as if trying to get the lie of the land.

They look into each other's eyes as they take the first sip after clinking the cans together.

'If you like we can do it today,' the sedatoress says.

Gastón is embarrassed, because he doesn't understand what it is that the sedatoress is proposing, her gaze now sliding over towards Kitten as she indicates him with a raise of her eyebrows. Now that she has come clean, she is offering Gastón the chance to abandon the spectacle, to forget the ceremony, to end the dog's suffering once and for all.

'It'll be cheaper, too,' the sedatoress says, to get rid of any drama from the situation.

The sedatoress watches, as do we, how Gastón leans back against the carob tree, gripping his can of beer hard.

'I'm not ready yet,' he says.

33

Pol's grandfather gets up in exasperation and walks across the restaurant to charge his phone, leaning on the bar with his elbows. Ever since he arrived, his days have consisted of having coded conversations with one-time collaborators and exchanging messages with supposed allies who might help him to resolve the misunderstanding. This is what Max's father calls the disappearance of 40 per cent of the public works budget from the coffers of the city council where he used to work: the misunderstanding.

In the dining area, sitting in the gloom, Gastón, Pol and Max still remain. Despite how fanciful everything Pol is saying sounds, we don't think he's lying; this is something far more sophisticated than a lie. So far, this is what we, along with Gastón, imagine: that Pol knows a lot, that his head is full of information; that the inhuman conditions of the Tundra have broken him, leading to an overdose of stress hormones, and that the way this alienation is manifesting is as an attack of paranoia. He is muddled by the fact that the investigations he is taking part in are, for trivial reasons (investment, patents, financial returns) confidential, and sees instead other objectives, secret ones, as if someone were writing a plot with hidden intentions; the origin of the conspiracy.

Gastón tries to calm him down by questioning him as you would a child, as a teacher would; he knows he cannot force him to return to normality, that it is Pol who must realise, on his own, how confused he is. He needs to believe that this crisis the boy is going through is something fleeting. And he entertains the hopeful thought that this episode could help Max, by reinstating the parental bond.

'Tell us everything,' Gastón says to Pol, 'from the beginning. There's no rush, we've got all the time in the world to listen to you.'

This is true, and the state of the restaurant confirms it: the tables that haven't been used in the last few days are covered with a fine layer of dust; two beer barrels are blocking the corridor that connects the bar with the dining area; the blackboard continues to offer the specials from the last day Max opened; in its destitute state, the restaurant gives off that stale, dirty smell that by now is also Max's characteristic odour; time appears to have stopped, as if this were Max's strategy for solving his problems, believing that this way the end of the month will never arrive, contradicting the laws of physics, as if the passage of time and the expansion of space were not the condition of all existence, as if the North Easterners were not out there, waiting.

Time has stopped mattering; there is too much time, they have nothing to do, so they are going to listen to everything Pol has to tell them.

'OK then,' Pol says, trying to work out where to begin.

He's shivering a little, although the air is not cold, warmed as it is by the room having been shut up for so long and by the heat emanating from the four human bodies and the one canine one as they gently metabolise.

'There is a theory – a hypothesis,' Pol corrects himself, 'called panspermia. Seeds everywhere. That's what panspermia means – that there are seeds of life throughout the whole universe. Not just on our planet. Not too long ago we believed that the conditions on Earth were unique or, at the very least, special.'

Pol pauses briefly, as if to indicate a full stop and a new line, the end of a paragraph, the end of the introduction. He drains the rest of the beer he'd been drinking with his meal. Then he continues.

He says that, in the last few years, probes, telescopes and spaceships have proved that this is not the case: in fact, the opposite is true and there is an endless number of places in the universe with conditions similar to those on Earth: a solid surface and some kind of atmosphere; being at a habitable orbiting distance from a star, as we are from the sun; and having an abundance of chemical elements in a liquid state which might, at some point, trigger the beginning of biological metabolism.

'One hypothesis of the origins of life on Earth,' Pol continues, 'says just that: that our seeds arrived from outer space.'

Lithopanspermia, Pol says. That these seeds of life arrived on a meteorite. Microlithopanspermia: that microbial life might have travelled on specks of dust through space. Radiopanspermia: spores of life that crossed the universe driven by radiation pressure from stars. Necropanspermia: inactive viruses, fragments of inert bacteria, which, when they arrived on Earth, came back to life.

'Or, the thing they're hiding from us. . . ' Pol says.

He pauses dramatically because, as well as being a scientist, he has seen, just as we have, too many films. He knows that this is the moment where the tension in his story reaches its limit, the climax prior to the big reveal. He gets up, walks to the bar, and comes back sipping from a fresh bottle of beer.

'Directed panspermia,' he says, still standing, with no intention of sitting back down. 'A colonisation carried out by an extraterrestrial civilisation which sent genetic material down to Earth.'

Gastón and Max stare at him, entranced. Paranoia always has a devastating logic to it, with no cracks, a logic that denies chance or coincidence and seeks to reveal a hidden order, the identity of the author of the plot, their secret intentions; all false, a mistake born of reading too much into things. But there are also paranoid people who are right – we've all met one, haven't we?

'We all come from up there,' Pol says, pointing with his bottle up at the ceiling of the restaurant.

He takes a long gulp of beer.

'We're an experiment,' he says.

Another gulp, as if summoning courage.

'We are all extraterrestrials.'

34

The panspermia stuff is real, Gastón confirms on the internet, as he searches on his phone once he's in bed. The concept exists, we mean, and all the variants that Pol explained. They are theories that are circulating equally among astrobiologists, with scepticism, and among fans of all things extraterrestrial, who defend them ardently. Some say that the Earth is a huge zoo protected by a superior alien civilisation.

Gastón also reads that there is a society of 'unknown beings' which secretly conducts world matters, which controls this experiment called life on Earth, and who others call 'unknown agents' or 'unknown superiors'. He would have carried on reading, but decides to stop when a virus alert pops up when he tries to click on the testimony of a supposed contactee.

He closes the browser on his phone and sends a message to Max. He asks if he is asleep yet, if he can give him a ring. Gastón sees on the screen of his phone that Max has read the message but isn't replying. He waits a couple of minutes and decides to take the initiative.

'Is something wrong?' Max says, when he picks up. 'Is Kitten all right?'

Gastón tells him that he wants to talk about Pol, and Max replies that he'll soon get over it, will realise he's not making any sense, and that the conditions in the Tundra were really tough but his son is reasonable and will see sense again. He says that Pol's boss told him these kinds of things did tend to happen and that they had to give him time to get back to normal.

'Did you tell him Pol's here?' Gastón asks.

'Not yet,' Max replies. 'Pol asked me not to say anything. He was very clear about that. You've seen how he is. I don't want to drive him away.'

Gastón stays silent to make the moment last longer. The phone held against his right ear heats it up ever so slightly; it is a feeling of well-being. The warm bed. His warm ear. Max's voice.

'Are you feeling better?' he asks. 'I could come by tomorrow afternoon to help you clear out the kitchen.'

Max also takes a while to reply. He will have his reasons, but we cannot know them, because we haven't been given access to him, to his thoughts and motivations. If we were to accompany him, instead of Gastón, we would be telling another story, a totally different one – far fewer things would happen, there wouldn't be as many characters, and we'd be suffering from serious claustrophobia by this point.

'Hey,' Max replies, avoiding once more the subject of the restaurant handover, which, if we analyse his behaviour up to now, he appears to find tedious, like the subplot of a novel that the narrator idly abandons, or a bad habit you try to make disappear by denying it exists.

Gastón waits. Although we can't see him, we can sense Max at the other end of the line, hesitating, weighing things up, trying to select the right words to get rid of Gastón, to evade his friend yet again without sounding rude. But when he does speak, he changes the subject.

'Did you get around to applying for planning permission for the market garden?' he asks.

'No,' Gastón replies.

'Well, you should do it,' Max says.

They say goodbye and Gastón, who has understood the proposal hidden behind Max's question, ends the call hurriedly, so as not to plunge headlong into making a promise, so as not to offer Max something he's not sure he's able to keep his word on, so as not to anticipate, here, something that, were it to come to fruition, would take place on future pages. It's not that Gastón wants to create suspense or intrigue, but now he has a plan – a plan B. And the fantasy of this plan excites him so much that it stops him from sleeping. He spends a few hours dreaming, with his eyes open, lying in the darkness, telling himself a happy little story as he listens to his own breathing and that of the dog, who is lying on his little bed next to Gastón's, and he realises that hope is just as deceptive as paranoia: both grow endlessly, perfect, invincible, until they bump up against reality, inexorable reality. But Gastón has always felt he would rather be a dreamer than bitter (luckily for us), and the only thing that slightly clouds this image of happiness is knowing that Kitten will not be there to share it with him.

35

Another string of messages from the past, from the Southern Cone. Gastón reads them as he stands in the kitchen, waiting for the water in the coffee pot to boil. They're from another number, a new number to block, we predict, if we use Gastón's previous behaviour as the basis for our prediction. In essence, they say the same as the messages from last time, except for the first one, the preamble, which starts off by asking if Gastón has received the messages from his other cousin, the brother of the one who's writing now. Then an identical litany: the injustice of the inheritance, how disproportionate it is, the devaluation, the assets, the demand for restitution, for a mutual agreement, a friendly one, with the whole of the family.

We already know what Gastón will do next. We are not wrong.

36

Using the native language, the estate agent tells his colleague that he's going out for a coffee with a client. He picks up the mobile phone next to his keyboard, steps out from behind the desk and walks determinedly towards the door. Gastón takes a while to react, as does Kitten, who has only just curled up on the ground in a ball.

It's the time when the schools finish for the day, and they have to dodge grandparents walking hesitantly and unruly children scattering crumbs of bread and biscuits all over the pavements. They walk past several coffee bars without stopping; Gastón supposes that the agent has his favourite, but he ends up taking him to a piece of waste ground that serves as a car park. There is no one else there; several of the cars have thick layers of dust on them, their tyres flat. The agent asks him to wait, walks over to an old two-door, opens it and returns with a pack of cigarettes in his hands.

'Do you smoke?' he asks.

Gastón says that he doesn't. The agent has to go back to the car to look for a lighter.

'This sort of thing isn't easy,' he says, after blowing out a succession of smoke rings, 'but it can be done. I'll have to pull some strings locally, get a councillor on side. Is it a dwelling you want to build?' he asks.

'No,' Gastón replies, 'a restaurant, something small; three hundred square feet max, at the entrance to the market garden.'

The agent tells him that it's not worth it for something that small – he could build something residential there, an apartment building, with a pool, green spaces, a playground for kids.

'If you built that here,' says the agent, 'in this neighbourhood, it'd make a real splash. It'd be your ticket to a luxury retirement.'

Curious, Gastón looks at the agent for the first time, noticing the sheen on his green tie, and tries to stop automatically linking him to Pol, to separate him from this mass of friends and classmates, all more or less the same: straightforward youths, middle-class boys content with their fate, speakers of the native language as a social leveller, football fans, fans of the city team, of the best footballer on Earth. He didn't expect him to be the one who would start testing all his hopes and dreams, or indeed, without being too dramatic about it, to place obstacles in his way. He thought that the kid might be his accomplice, but he realises now that the green tie symbolises far more than a precarious job with the possibility of making a killing once in a while.

'Look at this,' the agent says, gesturing around him with his half-smoked cigarette. 'Can you believe it? This is more than six and a half thousand square feet. It belongs to the council – they seized it when the new urban development plan was made, that whole mess with the nature reserves.'

He pauses to finish smoking his cigarette.

'Have you ever come here at night?' he asks. 'Do you know what this reserve is for?'

As if he knew exactly what he had to do, Kitten starts to moan and writhe around in pain. He's a good companion, Kitten; intelligent, always has been. Gastón would swear that he's pretending, but this time the attack is more violent, much longer. The agent stares at the scene indifferently, as if, instead of a dog in pain, what he was witnessing was a child's tantrum.

'I have to go,' Gastón tells the agent, after explaining to him what's wrong with the dog once the animal calms down again.

'Think about it,' the agent says. 'Do it for Pol, he's gonna need a lot of help now that he's lost his mind.'

'What?' Gastón asks.

The agent gives him a condescending look, as if he were the older man and Gastón the young one, and lights a second cigarette.

'Don't be offended,' he says. 'I've got a sister with schizophrenia. There are places by the sea with gardens, where they get all the help they need. But they're private. They cost a lot of money. I only wish I were in your position.'

Gastón turns his back on the man and tugs hard on Kitten's lead so that they can get away, but the dog's slow, wary reaction forces him to carry on listening.

'My girlfriend is friends with Ona,' the agent explains; 'Pol's ex. You've no idea, he just flipped – they were so scared they called the police.'

37

As he walks back to the market garden he is slowly overcome by a paranoid fantasy, each step triggering one more argument in support of his fears. What if Pol has gone mad? What if he is unhinged? Who can have unhinged him? Ancient legends tell of supernatural beings who make their victims lose their minds by touching their heads with a finger, but Pol is a scientist, and Gastón does not believe in such things. What has unhinged Pol, if anything has, are the inhuman conditions of the Tundra, the stress that has turned into anxiety attacks, perhaps a psychotic episode. What if Pol ends up turning into the new neighbourhood madman?

There used to be other mad people. The old woman who would stop passers-by to offer them drawings she took from a binder with the gas company's logo on it; a young lad who would wave his hands around while shouting and arguing with an imaginary enemy; various destitute people who camped out next to cashpoints in the bad weather and had spots in the squares when it was fine; another one who was pretty famous, many, many years ago, Gastón recalls, when the Historic Park was being renovated, a guy who used to give orders to the workers because he said he was a city councillor; and the dog woman, of course, the one who spent her days stroking dogs, who Gastón knew really well because she loved Kitten (a love he returned), and who one day just disappeared without a trace.

He pauses and sits down at a table outside a bar, Kitten at his feet, dozing. He asks for a beer and takes his phone from his pocket. Stress hormones are the body's response to a threatening situation, psychological or physical, fictitious or real, Gastón reads on a medical information site. Genetic inheritance might predispose someone to a greater vulnerability, which could produce episodes of psychosis, depression, or anxiety disorders. Delirium or hallucinations are related to schizophrenia or bipolar disorder, and an acute response speeds up physiological processes such as breathing, as well as heart rate and blood pressure; as these increase, it's as if the body were preparing for a climax, for some kind of outcome, although in reality this feeling is constant, because one of the things that mental imbalance alters is the perception of time (it cancels out past and future, fusing them with the present). There is no cause or effect: everything happens at the same time, in an eternal present where reality appears complete. Gastón types in the words 'cold', 'shivering' and 'body temperature', but doesn't get any conclusive results.

He has sat down at the terrace of a Far Eastern bar; he only realises now, when the Far Easterner places his glass on the table, along with a little dish of toasted maize. Gastón takes a long drink of beer, to try and dull his paranoia, to still his racing thoughts, the logic of symptoms and effects that make him fear for Pol's mental health. It's just a temporary episode, Gastón says to himself, like a suspected tragedy that is later ruled out for being implausible or inconsistent, unless genetics demands that it continue. But how to find out what Max's family's heredity is, and, more difficult still, that of Pol's mother?

'What's wrong with your dog?' Gastón hears someone say, suddenly.

It's the Far Easterner who has said it, making a super-human effort to pronounce the word 'wrong', pointing with his right hand towards the spot on the floor where Kitten is lying, towards the pool of blood he has left, all around his tail, on the flowery pavement tiles. Gastón rushes to pick up his serviette, but the Far Easterner gets there first.

'Don't worry,' he says, 'I'll clean it up for you.'

38

When the sedatoress opens her case this time, as well as the syringes and the surgical tape, we see four red cans.

'Drinks are on me today,' she says to Gastón, holding out her right arm to offer him a can.

Gastón thanks her and opens his beer right away. The sedatoress waits until she's finished administering the opiate, until she's confirmed the effect on Kitten and checked his pulse. She sits down, leaning against the carob tree, and strokes the dog's back with her left hand. Today she has come a little later, and the play of light and shadow under the tree obscures the lines of the spider vein on her cheek, lines that today seem more purple than red.

'How long have you had this place?' she asks, looking over at the neighbouring plot where the elongated onions are growing, and at the one behind it, which has some tiny cabbages in it.

'Nearly thirty years,' Gastón replies.

'I thought you were younger,' the sedatoress says, pulling a wry face to underline the irony of the compliment. 'Do you have a family?'

Gastón says that he doesn't.

'Bit of a loner, are you?' the sedatoress says. 'What I mean is, you must spend a lot of time on your own – don't you get bored?'

Even though they might seem rude, the sedatoress's words do not bother Gastón, who is actually grateful for the curiosity of his new companion. He has missed chatting, telling someone about his day, ever since Max became locked away inside himself. Gastón says no, that the market garden demands he stick to a pretty strict routine. He doesn't have any spare time.

'But don't get the wrong idea,' he says. 'I do have friends, and some of them are so close you could say they're like my family. Well, they are my family,' he corrects himself, on the spot, to emphasise his conviction.

He tells her about Max and Pol, with an enthusiasm the sedatoress finds touching, we realise, because she abandons her ironic tone and listens intently to him.

'Did you never get married?' she asks, when Gastón pauses to take a sip of his beer. 'Or are you and your friend a couple? Sorry – maybe I didn't understand.'

Gastón laughs at the misunderstanding. He tells her the story of Pol's mother, of Max's multiple love affairs, dozens in the years he's known his friend, relationships of a few days or weeks or, at most, a few months. The sedatoress asks if Gastón is also one of those 'incorrigible bachelors', and the phrase is so twentieth century that it makes us wonder about her age – is she older than she looks?

'Not really, no,' Gastón replies. 'That's not really my style.'

They have finished their first beer, and the sedatoress takes the two others from her case, one for each of them. Then Gastón tells her about crop cycles, the seasons, the weather, the rain, the watering and the irrigation; the time measured out in harvests, the solitude, the company of Kitten;

the routine, the mechanical, automatic activities, repeated thousands of times for so many years; the blights, the caterpillars, the mice; about his grandfather, in the Southern Cone, who also had a market garden, about the fig trees of his childhood, and about the time when Max bought pepper seeds from his homeland and they turned out to be so spicy that they had to scrap the entire crop because no one could cope with the heat.

'And you've given me this whole spiel just to avoid telling me whether you've got a partner?' the sedatoress asks, in joking mode once again. 'Highly suspicious, if you ask me.'

Gastón forces a smile and stares at the spider vein on the woman's right cheek.

'What about you?' he replies. 'Tell me something about you – this is starting to feel like an interrogation.'

He puts the empty beer can from which he has been sipping down on the ground and crushes it with his right foot.

'Shall we have another?' the sedatoress asks.

39

Gastón and Pol hear the lawyer from the country say that there are places where Far Eastern budget bazaars have been banned. He says that last Christmas, in the Tundra of the Far West, there was a public health issue, caused by some soft toys that had become popular.

'They're called Mogwai,' the lawyer from the country says. 'Did any of you hear anything about that? See it on the news?'

The people in the audience say that they didn't. Gastón and Pol don't say a word, so as not to be rumbled: they have stopped in the doorway to the room where the meeting is being held, in the back of a traditional local business, shielded by the half-open door. This time Kitten isn't with them, which means that Gastón foresaw this scene, the stealthy eavesdropping, and chose not to risk the dog giving them away. Seeing Gastón away from the market garden without Kitten is strange; accustomed as we are to always seeing them together, it conveys an image of something incomplete, a face without nose or eyes.

He is relieved that so few people have responded to the call; he pokes his head round the door and counts just six people in the audience. He recognises the man from the Cordillera and his friend, the Pacific Coast Guy. Not even El

Tucu is here. Gastón received the invitation on his phone via the instant messaging app and would have ignored it completely had Pol not come to him with some story about El Tucu telling him they'd be discussing Max's situation and efforts to save the restaurant. It concerns Gastón that El Tucu is now badgering Pol. This is what we understand: that since neither Max nor Gastón have taken any notice of El Tucu, he has now gone after the boy.

'Of course you didn't,' the lawyer from the country continues, 'because the Far Easterners don't want you to know.'

He says the Far Easterners put a lot of money into controlling the media, manipulating public opinion, spreading fake news. He explains that the Mogwai are stuffed animals that look similar to bears, but with some catlike features. He says the poor quality of the materials and a particular toxic chemical product used in their manufacture led to an epidemic of allergies, and that dozens of children died from anaphylactic shock (we're the ones who say 'anaphylactic shock'; the lawyer from the country repeats the word 'allergy').

'A friend of mine who works at the port here told me there's a shipment of these monsters ready to be sent out to all the budget bazaars in the city. No one will do anything. You'll see. No one will do anything until it's too late – until children start dying. Our children. Our grandchildren.'

The lawyer from the country pauses in his speech, and so Gastón quickly asks Pol if he's going to stay or wants to go in. He, Gastón, has had enough already. He was afraid he'd encounter a horde of residents prepared to start an ethnic cleansing war, but instead what he sees here looks more like the monthly meeting of a conspiracy theorists' club.

'I'm going to go,' Gastón says. 'I don't like leaving Kitten alone in the house.'

'Come on then,' Pol replies.

They walk back through the shop to the street, and as soon as they step onto the pavement they bump into El Tucu.

'Is the meeting over already?' El Tucu asks Pol.

'No,' Pol says, 'but we can't stay.'

'I'll report back later,' El Tucu says. 'We're going to help your father out, you'll see.'

He slaps Pol on the shoulder by way of a goodbye, without looking at Gastón, and goes into the shop. It was an utterly patronising slap – El Tucu used just the right amount of force to give Pol the sense that he is older than him and, most importantly, that he knows much more about life. Before Gastón can tell Pol that he needs to be careful, Max's son speaks first.

'Tell me about the sedatoress,' he says.

'Are you coming to mine for dinner?' Gastón replies. 'I've got freshly picked courgettes. I'll grill them with some olive oil and we'll make a pasta sauce – sound good?'

'You don't need to convince me,' Pol says. 'I'm sick of eating old food out of Tupperware at the restaurant.'

They set off towards Gastón's house at a pace; Pol tends to walk fast anyway, and Gastón is nervous because he's worried Kitten might have another attack in his absence.

They round the corner of the street Max's restaurant is on, and as they get closer they make out a man leaning against the door, who seems to be looking up, down and to both sides, as if monitoring the building and everyone who walks past it. When he sees him, Pol turns around to retrace his steps.

'Not this way,' he says.

Gastón tries to see who the man is.

'What's wrong, who is it?' he asks Pol, going after him.

He takes him by the arm to try and stop him, but Pol shakes him off.

'Let's go up this way,' Pol says; 'I'll tell you later.'

40

'Who was that guy?' Gastón asks, eventually.

They're in the kitchen, finishing off the washing-up and drinking their third beer. Gastón chose to put off this conversation so they could have a nice, relaxed dinner together; he has missed the boy so much that he's decided that solving the mystery, talking about the situation with the restaurant, with Max, Pol's grandfather, Kitten's health, Pol running away from the Tundra and what happened at Mariona's house – all that can wait. That merits waiting. They have spoken about the crops on Gastón's land, about the city team, its chances of winning the continental championship, the health of the best footballer on Earth and about how tasty the courgettes were.

'You believe me, right?' Pol asks.

Gastón is silent as he wipes a plate with a tea towel to dry it off. He does it thoroughly, polishing the wear on it, the scratches caused by the movement of knives, which have scored a latticework of fine grooves into the surface of all his plates. He is artificially prolonging the moment, because cleaning up after dinner for two is something easily finished in a matter of minutes. Gastón wants some more time to think about how he's going to tackle this conversation that's been put off, not just today, but ever since the day Pol told them the reasons why he had run away from his work in the Tundra. We don't know if he believes the boy or not. He doesn't know if he believes him or not. And we don't know if we should believe him, either.

'I didn't tell you everything the other day,' Pol says. He approves of Gastón's silence and seems to be reading his thoughts. 'Shall we have some coffee?'

Gastón puts the coffee pot on the stove. They finish clearing up and wait in silence for it to percolate. Both want to have this conversation in ideal conditions, sitting on the living room sofa, pretending that nothing is wrong. We suppose Pol must think that, this way, there's more of a chance Gastón will believe him, if he lays out his arguments calmly. Gastón, meanwhile, just longs for normality, to not have to admit that his fears and the estate agent were right.

They pour the coffee into little cups and move to the living room, treading carefully so as not to spill anything, just as they will have to tread carefully in the conversation, Gastón thinks, so that it doesn't spill over into dangerous territory. Gastón sits down on the sofa; Pol sits on the floor, next to Kitten, who is stretched out on his little bed by the table, where an ancient TV sits.

'I didn't say any more the other day because my grand-father's such a pain the neck,' Pol says. 'You and Dad didn't exactly back me up, either.'

Gastón merely raises his eyebrows, figuring that this will suffice to make Pol understand that no one is prepared to react the right way to a revelation such as this one. No matter how many films a person has seen, how many books of science fiction they have read, no one is prepared to confront something like this in reality.

'Someone programmed this experiment,' Pol starts to explain. 'Directed panspermia,' he clarifies, in case Gastón (and we) have forgotten. 'It wasn't a spontaneous thing, it wasn't that someone just said, "Let's see what happens if we send these seeds of life to Earth." They knew what was going to happen, they predicted it, they planned it. Do you understand what I'm trying to say?'

He pauses to take a sip of his coffee.

'It was a colonisation,' he adds.

Neither Gastón nor we are sure how keen he or we are to accept the logic of Pol's arguments. What we want, in actual fact, what we would like – what Gastón longs for – is for Pol to stop talking now, for him not to go any further, not to force us to reach the conclusion that the nervous breakdown he is experiencing is serious and that he might perhaps require medication and institutionalisation. A ball of fire settles in Gastón's chest; he is scared.

'Pol,' he starts to say, to interrupt him, to steer the conversation somewhere else, towards a more traditional comedy of manners, but it is Pol who interrupts him.

'Let me speak – you're the only one I can tell this to, no one else.'

Gastón acquiesces, with his eyelashes, a slight closing and opening of his eyes that is a promise of patience, of empathy, evidence of the mutual understanding developed over the years as he watched Pol grow up and which, even though it's not what Pol hopes for – a sign that he believes in him unquestioningly – is now something far more profound, a promise of loyalty: that Gastón will listen to him and will, whatever happens, be there by his side.

'It all started in a little pool of water,' Pol says, 'in the presence of light and heat, where these seeds started to undergo complex variations.'

As Pol sets out his theory of evolution, the way these 'extraterrestrial seeds' gave rise to cells, as he talks of amino acids and proteins, of the long metabolic journey that culminated in beings controlled by hormones, mixing concepts he learnt as a student in the Biology department with ideas that seem to have come from science fiction, he doesn't look at Gastón – he looks at Kitten, stroking the dog's back, and this really worries us. Pol is embarrassed by what he is saying; Pol knows that what he is saying is absurd and yet, even so, Pol believes it to be true.

'And what does all that have to do with the guy we saw by the restaurant?' Gastón asks.

'He's my boss,' Pol replies. 'He was my boss, in the Tundra,' he corrects himself. 'He's here for me. He wants to make sure I'm not going to tell anyone about what I discovered.'

Gastón swallows, preparing himself for the revelation, although we fear that what Pol says is going to become even more fanciful, move even closer to fiction, impervious to the categories of truth or lie. If we were to reach that point we would be doomed to accept anything, and perhaps we can do this, if there is enough verisimilitude involved, for the sake of entertainment, in order to get to the end, to the last page, but for Gastón things are more complicated; he would not be breaking with realism, like we would; he would be breaking with reality.

'The equipment they're developing in the Tundra has two uses,' Pol starts to explain, by this point excluding himself from the responsibility of his own participation. 'It's not just to look for life on other planets. They want to take it there, too. Colonise one of the frozen moons. It's humanity's directed panspermia project, you see? We're going to plant our own seeds on those moons, we're going to get into the war of space colonisation, into universal imperialism,' he says, reverting to the plural that now includes not only the research team out in the Tundra, but also Pol and Gastón, us, all terrestrial beings.

'And how are we going to survive, buried in the ice?' Gastón asks, desperately trying to get Pol to see the contradictions in his tale.

'There's water underneath the ice,' Pol says. 'This war is fought over a scale of millions of years; in theory, one day the conditions on these moons will change and they'll be able to support life. When that moment comes, our seeds will be there, ready to develop into life.'

'War?' Gastón replies. 'Against who?'

'This is all political,' Pol says. 'Don't you see?'

Gastón shrugs, because in truth he can't follow the ever-changing direction of Pol's rambling speech.

'Whose side are you on?' Pol asks. 'The side of the ones who think that everyone should know this, or the ones who think it should be hidden, kept secret, in the hands of a small elite of initiates?'

The side of the ones who think that this is all a paranoid delusion, Gastón thinks; but he says nothing.

41

He walks Pol home, with Kitten still half asleep and not understanding the reason for this walk at the crack of dawn, considering that his daily routine of bowel movements has already been completed. He has told the boy that he wants to make sure he gets home all right and that the older man doesn't intercept him, and it's partly true, although really his plan is to speak to Max.

They make the journey without mishap, and after watching Pol go into the building and walk to the lift Gastón presses the little portable control that opens the restaurant's shutters. As expected, Max is still there despite the late hour, sitting at the bar, his head bent over his phone, devoted to his reverie of multicoloured sweeties. Pol's grandfather is sitting on the other side of the bar, also concentrating on his phone, waiting for news that might absolve him, we imagine, or rereading messages he's received to try and decide whether any of them contain a double meaning or a hidden clue.

'We've got to do something about Pol,' Gastón says, when the shutters have finished their descent and the entrance to the restaurant is closed.

Kitten tries to walk over to his favourite spot by the bar, between two stools, but Gastón stops him, letting him know that it will be a short conversation; the dog, however, is sleepy, and flops down right there, at Gastón's feet. As neither Max nor his father says anything (they don't even look up from their phones), Gastón summarises what he has just talked about with Pol, the boy's conspiracy theories, and ventures a few diagnoses: depression, anxiety, a psychotic episode, schizophrenia —

'We all go through bad patches,' Max replies vehemently, interrupting Gastón's list.

He doesn't lift his head, and the gleam from the multi-coloured sweeties makes us think that he is actually talking about himself, not Pol.

'What if it's not just something short-term?' Gastón asks.

'He'll get over it,' Max replies. 'Don't you have any faith in him?'

Gastón says that people don't get over situations like this through force of will, pleas and advice, or motivational books; he might need therapy, medication; it might be something chemical or hormonal.

'Southern Conish people want to resolve everything on the therapist's couch,' Max says to Pol's grandfather.

'In any case,' Gastón says, ignoring Max's comment, 'we don't know what his genetic background is.'

He looks from Max to Pol's grandfather, as if to emphasise that what he has just said is somewhat euphemistic, because one of them is suffering from depression and the other is a textbook case of authoritarian megalomania.

'Your mother's crazy,' Pol's grandfather says to Max.

'And you're a psychopath,' Max replies.

The two start an argument that Gastón has heard a few times now and which he anticipated a few chapters ago, when Pol's grandfather showed up; it's what has happened every time Max's father has visited the city. When Gastón interrupts them, neither of the two insists on continuing; after so many years they are bored, tired of repeating the same things. He tells them that it's a given that the inhuman conditions of the Tundra led to the crisis Pol is currently going through, but that it's also important to rule out there being a genetic predisposition.

Gastón's phone buzzes in his trouser pocket; Max has sent him two contacts from his address book.

'That's my mother's number, and Pol's mother's sister's number,' says Max. 'Just don't get me involved in this.'

'What about your children, your grandchildren?' Gastón asks Max's grandfather.

'What about them?' Max's father says.

'Has there ever been a case of this kind of illness?' Gastón says.

'How should I know?!' Max's father replies.

42

It's the sedatoress who lets Gastón know, since he hasn't clocked it. Someone is knocking at the gate, calling out good afternoon, clapping their hands together. Gastón deposits the beer can by Kitten's flank, the animal still contentedly sleeping his morphine sleep; he leaves the protective shade of the carob tree and walks up the path that leads to the entrance to the market garden. As he gets closer, he feels a little disappointed when he realises that it's not Pol, who has promised to drop by one day at this sort of time so that Gastón can introduce him to the sedatoress.

It's an older man who looks vaguely familiar, and who he only identifies when it's already too late to think better of it and turn round, although he does manage to stop walking a few feet before the gate so that the other man can see that he is not going to let him in. It's Pol's boss from the Tundra, the man we saw yesterday by the entrance to the restaurant.

The older man introduces himself, but before he can explain the reason for his visit Gastón cuts in.

'How did you find me here?' he asks.

'Pol was always telling us about this market garden,' the older man replies, in an attempt at playing the sentimental card, or perhaps just telling the truth. 'The restaurant's closed;

I didn't get any answer at his father's house, either. I asked around and one of his neighbours told me how to get here.'

Gastón's body asks him to turn his back on the man and walk down the slope to get back to the sedatoress, to be at Kitten's side, the place he should be at this moment. His head, however, starts to ask questions. What if what Pol told him wasn't a fantasy? What if at least part of it is true? What if the older man is here, on this page, with secret, dark motivations, which we aren't yet able to understand?

'What are you doing here?' Gastón asks him.

We know it's highly unlikely that the older man will tell him the truth, the whole truth, but he will at least tell his version, and this alone is important, so that we can contrast it with Pol's.

'I'll be honest,' the older man says, and Gastón prepares himself for one of two things: a lie, or a load of nonsense, 'this isn't just about Pablo, it goes further than that.'

The fact that the older man says 'Pablo' surprises us, but Gastón is used to it, he doesn't even notice the difference between people calling him Pablo, in the colonising language, or Pol, in the native language. The older man pauses and looks at the lock on the gate, hoping that his promise to be sincere will shift Gastón's attitude, that he will open the gate and invite him in. But the only thing that Gastón shifts is the weight of his body, from one foot to the other.

'I head up a group of researchers,' continues the older man, resigning himself to Gastón's distrust. 'I'm responsible for managing some of the funds, it's me who reports back to the investors.'

All at once, Gastón loses interest, because he can guess what the older man is going to say next. That Pol running away has compromised the group's work, that the investors

127

will write a negative report, that there's a risk they will put the project's financing on hold. Which is indeed what he goes on to say, give or take a word.

'I shouldn't be telling you this,' the older man adds, 'but we're under quite a lot of pressure right now – some of the investors aren't happy.'

This last bit of specific detail, which aims to add a finishing touch of plausibility to the older man's story, irritates Gastón. It makes him angry that he has chosen the shortcut of sincerity, this pragmatic tale of investors, projects and funding, instead of first attempting some empathy, instead of feigning – even if just out of good grace – concern about Pol, about his disappearance and his mental health. Despite how hypocritical a sentimental approach would have seemed to us, this is what we would have expected, too; but the older man is in a hurry, we realise, and has no time for empathy or tact.

This time Gastón does obey his body and, without saying goodbye, heads back down the path that leads through the beds of vegetables towards the carob tree, ignoring the older man calling out to him.

'Is something wrong?' the sedatoress asks, displaying her keen sense of hearing, listening to the older man's shouts.

'A guy I owe money to,' Gastón lies, a convincing lie. 'You're going to have to wait until he gets bored and buggers off.'

'Give us another beer, then,' the sedatoress says, holding out her empty can.

43

That evening, there's a message from Pol on Gastón's phone. He reads it in the kitchen as he keeps one eye on a pot with a handful of green beans boiling away. Pol tells him not to come to the restaurant, today or tomorrow, or in the next few days, and not to come looking for them (neither him nor Max), until he, Pol, lets him know that it's OK. He says that his boss, the older man, is loitering around the restaurant, and has found a spot nearby to keep watch. Pol doesn't think the man will be able to stay for too long, to leave the research group unsupervised, that he'll have to return to the Tundra soon, and they'll just have to wait until he gives up.

'We have to start clearing out the restaurant,' Gastón replies. 'We can't wait any longer, we're going to run out of time.'

He finishes preparing the beans, some scrambled eggs, eats dinner; he showers and then goes to bed.

Pol does not reply.

He thinks that tomorrow, without fail, he will have to go and speak to the North Easterner to ask him to extend the handover period for the restaurant.

Before closing his eyes, he tries once more.

'There's a game tomorrow,' he writes.

But he gets no reply from Pol.

44

He takes a seat on one of the wooden benches in the Square of the Revolutionary Women, as if he were resting, or letting Kitten have a breather. It's the hour when the office workers finish for the day, later than the period when the school-children and their grandparents fill the square, although there are still a few of them here and there, prolonging the afternoon, the kids having tantrums to put off going home. Gastón watches the pedestrians crossing the square diagonally to save themselves a few feet of walking. He trusts that fate, or the extraordinary, will not prevent routine from being observed. He knows that Mariona, Pol's ex, passes by here every weekday, on her way home from the office; he has seen her many times, has waved at her from afar, and occasionally she comes over to stroke Kitten and exchange a few polite words with Gastón.

This time she takes longer than Gastón has calculated, but she does appear, although not on her own; she is with a friend he doesn't recognise. Gastón gets to his feet and goes to meet her without pretending it's a coincidence; there's no need to, and he believes his concern gives him the right to question her. He says hello and asks if he can speak to her for a moment, throwing a furtive but friendly glance at her friend, as if excusing himself for being rude. Mariona says goodbye to her companion, a friend from the office, if we pay attention to their promise to see each other again the following morning.

'Coffee?' Gastón asks Mariona, as soon as the friend walks off.

'I didn't want to kick him out,' Mariona replies, 'but we got scared. Is he all right?'

She leaves her mouth half open, an expression that looks like anxiety to us, or guilt, or remorse, but as he stares at her exposed upper incisors, Gastón recalls what Pol told him and Max a couple of years ago, that when he and Mariona used to kiss they had to be really careful about the position of her jaws, because once they had got stuck together, the set of teeth in one jaw locked to the set in the other, like pieces of a puzzle, and could not be separated. It made the couple laugh hysterically, and they only managed to calm down because they were practically choking. They interpreted it as a sign that they were compatible, although in actual fact, Pol had explained to Gastón and his father, scientifically speaking, it happened because of the position of her upper right canine and his opposite lower one, which had become locked together.

She's a good person, Mariona, Gastón has always known it; he tended to think of her slightly uneasily because she belonged to that world Pol had never left; his school, the square, their neighbourhood. He always felt that Pol ought to expand that circle, meet other people, other realities, open himself up to the world, become more complex, grow stronger. The Tundra, of course, has turned out to be a trap: a frozen desert, a commune of eccentric people carrying out routine tasks while they type out abstract reports that only a handful of experts will be able to decipher, a place that is enough to send you crazy, quite literally.

Gastón says that Pol is acting a little strange at the moment, and that's why he wanted to speak to Mariona, to find out what happened.

'It was the heating,' Mariona replies. 'Me and my house-mate don't leave it on during the day, otherwise you can imagine what the bills would be like. But Pol would stay in the house all day long, and not only did he leave it on, he turned it up really high, as high as it would go. When we got back in the evening you couldn't breathe, it was like an oven. I live with two friends and we talked to him, but it was useless, he was always cold: he just sat there shivering, he would cling to me in bed and I couldn't sleep because it put me on edge, him clattering away like that. At first he went on the defensive, and then he accused me of not wanting to help him; he turned really aggressive and almost came to blows with one of my friend's boyfriends – she was the one who called the police when we asked him to leave, and Pol shut himself in my room and started shouting that we were all a bunch of traitors. He called us traitors – just think! I thought I'd go and tell his father, and so I went over to the restaurant, but it was shut; I think he's on holiday. Is Pol staying with you now?'

'Did he tell you why he decided to come back?' Gastón asks, not answering her question.

'We've all been screwed over, you know?' Mariona says, also following the reasoning dictated by her conscience and not that of Gastón's questions; it's like two worries in dialogue with each other. 'Why did Pol have to go so far away, to such an awful place? There are excellent research institutes here, some at his own university even, but he'll never be able to work there. It's just a few old fogies who've been sitting there keeping their seats warm since the Cambrian period.'

This is how you go from fear to animosity, Gastón thinks, sadly; this is how the metabolism of resentment is reinforced. We take advantage of these moments of reflection to look closely at Mariona: her clothes purchased in last year's sales, the hairband she uses to tie up her ponytail, almost certainly from the Far Eastern budget bazaar; her fake leather bag, the lack of make-up, like an expression of natural austerity, or of austere naturalness; in summary: her irresolute way of being in the world, which might seem like a choice, but is in fact the opposite, a lack of options, a lack of money, because in this world consumption is the means by which we differentiate ourselves.

She crouches down and gives Kitten a hug, and the dog lets her. It is a hug that lasts for several seconds, as if she were hugging not just the dog, but also Pol, Max and Gastón.

'Take care, little one,' Mariona says to the dog as she stands up, and she gives Gastón two kisses, one on each cheek, and then walks away.

45

'Yes,' the North Easterner says to Gastón.

Yes, there is something Gastón can do for him. He has just granted him and Max three more days to hand over the restaurant and is now, in exchange, asking Gastón to help him get to the stadium to watch a match played by the city team. He says that he wants to take his brother as a welcome gift, that he's tried to get tickets but there aren't any left.

Gastón's reaction to the North Easterner's request is a defensive one: why does the man think that he can get him tickets? Who has told him? And he starts to speculate, ever so slightly paranoid now, about who might have been blabbing – is it the owner of the Southern Cone restaurant? The father of the best footballer on Earth? Or can it have been the sports press, always needing to fill so many pages every day with any old nonsense? – until the North Easterner asks if he is from the same part of the Earth as the best footballer on Earth, revealing the logic behind his thought process, the reason why he thinks Gastón might be able to help him. Gastón replies that he will see what he can do, that he'll try and get hold of some tickets, ignoring the question about which part of the Earth he comes from.

The North Easterner's interest in football makes Gastón think that he could probably offer him the TV system from the restaurant, maybe help Max recoup some of his money this way. He sees his chance, but learns that Max has refused to have anything to do with the North Easterner.

'I tried to talk to him about all that,' the man says. 'We could use the furniture, too. Your friend did not want to listen.'

This is not an accusation, it's information. Gastón apologises on behalf of Max in any case, and explains that his friend is going through a bad patch, that it's been hard to get used to the idea of closing the restaurant.

'Remind me what you're called again?' the North Easterner asks.

Gastón reminds him of his name and then asks the North Easterner to remind him of his.

'I never told you,' the North Easterner says; 'you didn't ask.'

Before Gastón can attempt another apology, the North Easterner interjects.

'It's all right,' he says, 'I'm called Nikolai, but everyone calls me Niko.'

With this, he brings the conversation to a close and goes back to what he was doing when Gastón first walked into the greengrocer's – watching a video on his phone – but Gastón doesn't move. The North Easterner presses the pause button on the screen and looks up at Gastón, at us, who are, as ever, with him, witnessing everything over his shoulder.

'Is Varushka here?' Gastón asks.

'Varya?' Niko replies.

'I've got a little present for her,' Gastón explains, hurriedly, 'if it's all right with you.'

Niko shouts out the diminutive version of the little girl's name, and both men wait. The North Easterner goes back to his video, disengaging from the situation. The girl emerges from the back of the shop and Gastón says that he's brought her something. The North Easterner translates it into their language, without lifting his head, and Varushka runs over to Gastón and Kitten, who is lying at Gastón's feet at the end of the lead.

'Here you go,' he says, 'he loves these. You can feed them to him, like this.'

He shows her some little meat-flavoured sticks and holds one out to Kitten. The little girl takes over, and Kitten greedily gulps down the treats. When he's finished, he happily licks the girl's hand. Varushka laughs, the dog's rough tongue tickling her.

'That was a present for the dog,' Niko says.

'She likes it,' Gastón replies.

46

The photos come through on the instant messaging app from an unknown sender, a local number, and when he downloads them Gastón works out that it's Yu who's sent them (forwarded them, in fact, because they come from a mass mailing, from some sort of campaign). The glass front of the budget bazaar shattered, smashed to pieces, the sign splattered with black paint, and the words 'Mogwai' now written in red, very much not invisible letters, as if confirming that the threat has been carried out. There are pictures of other businesses, and a letter from the League of Far Eastern Traders calling for support from local people and intervention from the authorities.

Thirteen business were attacked in the early hours of the morning. Almost all are Far Eastern budget bazaars, and a couple of bars, a hairdresser's and a Near Eastern corner shop were also attacked. Gastón reads the survey of the damage in the paper, leaning his elbows on the bar in a traditional little café located on the avenue leading up towards the Historic Park as he waits for his coffee, Kitten dozing at his feet.

'Where do they get the money to buy up businesses?' the owner of the place asks, using the native language, when he sees that Gastón is interested in this piece of news. 'That's what they should be investigating.'

Gastón does not look up from the newspaper, choosing not to encourage the owner to continue; but the man, who now has his back to the bar as he waits for the coffee to finish dripping through, drones on.

'They buy everything, doesn't matter what it is,' he says, switching to the colonising language, assuming that Gastón is ignoring him because he doesn't speak the native language, 'businesses about to go bust or to be sold when the owners retire, and ones that are doing well, too, even if they cost a lot, if they're keen on the location. It's a ploy to take over the city. They won't go near me because I don't have outside space. If you haven't got a terrace they're not interested.'

The man puts Gastón's coffee down on the bar; it gives off a steam that is far too thick, and we can see the yellowish ring staining the inside of the cup, betraying the fact that it's burnt (the machine heats the water up more than recommended; it's not been properly calibrated). Gastón mentally reconstructs the chain of production and distribution that starts with a farmer tending his coffee plants on the slopes of the Southern Cone, or somewhere in the South East of the Earth; then the journey the harvested beans make to the East or the West, depending on where they come from, but always northwards, towards the roasters and the North Western middlemen; all culminating in this scalding liquid that Gastón should not ingest, if he wishes to avoid heartburn and acid reflux.

He asks for the bill. Pays. And leaves the bar without touching the cup.

47

He gives the little tuber a good rub to clean the earth off it and squeezes it between his first finger and thumb, to gauge how ripe it is. Then he studies its colour by the almost spring-like light of the morning, that light which took eight minutes to travel the distance separating us from the sun. He is crouching down, right in the middle of the potato patch between two rows of plants. He stands up, removes his gloves and takes his phone from his trouser pocket.

'The potatoes are ready,' he types, 'shall I bring you some?' He waits for the signal to complete its journey there and back, speculating as to whether the recipient is available and ready for him.

'Excellent,' we read, right away. 'I'll send word that you're coming.'

Gastón stands looking at the messages as if, as well as reading them, he needed to study them in search of something, a stimulus or an incentive of some sort. He hesitates; he feels something close to shame or embarrassment, and his central nervous system sends a message to his cheeks, which burn.

'Listen,' he writes, finally, 'I wouldn't want to bother you – you know I've never asked you for anything, but could you get hold of a couple of tickets for the next game? They're for someone I owe a really big favour to.'

'Of course, no problem,' we read, right away, and Gastón feels doubly relieved.

'Thank you so much,' he types, 'where can I collect them?'

'I'll send them to you now,' we read, 'and you can print them off.'

Gastón says thank you again, puts his phone away and his gloves back on, and then bends back down towards the earth and starts pulling up the potatoes from the same part of the Earth as the best footballer on Earth.

48

This time they do it in the shade of the tool shed's little veranda, because it's raining and the shade of the carob tree doesn't provide enough shelter. Kitten is already sleeping his happy sleep. Gastón and the sedatoress are having a beer and a few snacks. Crisps, some cured ham and some olives the sedatoress brought. Each day he feels more comfortable around her, although there are some things about her that nag at him, and Gastón isn't sure this is the moment to interrogate her. Why does he feel the need to know more about the sedatoress's life and what drives her? Is it just curiosity, or is there something else, something that is happening to Gastón, even though we don't quite dare, just yet, to name it?

'Why do you do this?' Gastón asks.

'Do what?' the sedatoress replies.

Gastón takes a sip of his beer to give him time to choose his words carefully.

'The whole ceremony,' he says, 'the sedatoress thing, the traditional healing – putting on a show of something you don't really believe in.'

'Don't get the idea you know me that well,' the sedatoress counters.

Gastón has avoided using more hurtful words, such as 'pretend' or 'fake', or 'lie', or 'deceive', but despite this, he's got it wrong. He feels bad, apologises to the sedatoress and immediately tries to make amends.

'The thing I'd like to know,' he says, 'is why you were honest with me.'

'You needed something else,' the sedatoress replies.

She is unruffled, not offended, and we can see that this is a conversation she is prepared for; she saw it coming, knew that sooner or later it would take place.

'And what did I need?' Gastón asks.

Here we are. We've arrived at the really big questions, but what Gastón couldn't have known is that the little game would turn against him. For a second Gastón, and we, too, fear that the sedatoress might pronounce one of those words that are so tremendous that we haven't dared write it up to now.

'Company, I suppose,' the sedatoress says.

Gastón is relieved at this answer and sees his chance to play down the importance of this conversation, to go back to that seemingly insubstantial moment made up of idle chatter, automatic movements, little gestures, unconscious actions and safe insignificance.

'Don't be so cheesy,' Gastón says, in a droll tone.

'What are you afraid of, Gastón?' the sedatoress replies.

They sit in silence, eating olives and throwing the stones into the next plot. Gastón could, while he does not reply to the sedatoress's question, make an effort to thread together the concepts that are now coming into his head, disjointedly; he does not do so, however, perhaps precisely because he is afraid.

'Maybe you'll get some olive trees,' the sedatoress says,

agreeing that it's time to return to light-hearted conversation.

'Do you believe in extraterrestrial life?' Gastón asks her.

49

There's no way of doing it nicely; Gastón knows this, and so it takes him a few days to get around to it. He has been reading up on how to do this on a range of medical sites, psychological and psychiatric, but despite all the tact he tries to inject into them, each message he types sounds (or reads, to be precise) like an insult.

Max's mother, who Gastón does not know because she has never come to the city (it's Max who visits her occasionally), does not reply. Gastón knows she has two other children (Max's half-siblings), and grandchildren as well; in any case, the fact that Max has a different father, and adding the partners of his mother's other children into the equation, perhaps there is already too much genetic information to get much of a clear sense of anything.

After a few hours, Pol's mother's sister replies. She says that she is tired of people saying her sister was crazy, and after so many years you'd think they might leave her to rest in peace. Her sister was a free woman, she says, she wasn't tied to anything and she didn't put up with hypocritical moralising, but she was not hysterical, and it wasn't like they were living in the stone age.

Gastón's first impulse is to call her to clear up the

misunderstanding, to properly explain what's going on with Pol; however, he realises that it's not his place, that he is not the one to go poking around in a wound that apparently (based on what we can read) has not healed. He replies that he has explained himself badly, that he is sorry and he won't bother her again.

50

He still hasn't had any news. Not from Max, or from Pol (not from anyone, in fact). Nobody replies to his messages, either; his calls go straight to answerphone. He worries that there's a problem with his phone, which has been doing some odd things recently: switched itself off, closed the browser. He decides to take it to be looked at.

He goes to one of the Near Eastern shops that specialise in repairing phones. It's just gone lunchtime and the place is empty; the old folk haven't woken up from their siestas yet, the children are still at school, and everyone else is still at work. Gastón explains to the Near Easterner exactly how the device is behaving. He's a young guy, who sucks his teeth grumpily like a Peninsular, as he opens and closes browsers and apps. He seems disappointed in Gastón, in his lack of skill or his technological ignorance, or perhaps in his temerity, in his lack of care or caution in using the phone.

The Near Easterner places the device on the glass counter and a snide little smile appears on his face.

'It's got a virus,' he says. 'You shouldn't look at those pages, this is what always happens.'

'Can you fix it?' Gastón asks, trying to dodge the Near Easterner's sermon, but the other man won't let it go.

'Porn sites, yeah? They're malicious, they try and steal information from your bank, your passwords.'

Suddenly embarrassed, Gastón looks behind him, checking that no one else has entered the shop. He asks again if the phone can be fixed.

'I can fix it,' the Near Easterner replies, 'but you can't go looking at these pages, 'cos the same thing's gonna happen again. And then you'll come back and complain I didn't do a good job. Or worse, your wife will come and I'll be the one who gets the telling-off. I can fix it, but there's no guarantee. I don't trust this stuff anymore. It only causes problems.'

Gastón asks him if the virus could have affected the way the apps work, because he hasn't received any messages for a while.

'It depends,' the man says. 'Gonorrhoea's not the same as syphilis, you get me? I'll have to check it first. Come back in two hours.'

The Near Easterner hands him a ticket. Gastón leaves the shop and decides to use the time to go and take a look at the restaurant.

He envisages the route he must take to get to the restaurant from further down, where he will be better protected; if he approaches it from higher up he'll have to cross the square and would be completely exposed, and in any case, as if that weren't enough, that's where the estate agent is. He can't take the main avenue because he'll run the risk of being intercepted by Pacific Coast Guy, but if he takes a right and heads uphill, to avoid the corner shop, he will then go past Cordillera Guy's internet café. Gastón is paralysed by doubt long enough for Kitten to grow bored and decide to flop down on the flowery pavement tiles. Without realising it (we realise it, though), Gastón is calculating who he would rather avoid, who it would be harder for him to evade, who is more dangerous.

He pulls on Kitten's lead to make the animal get up, and commands him to walk without choosing a direction. He wants the dog to decide for him and Kitten, of course, out of laziness, follows the way the ground slopes and starts walking down towards the avenue.

51

The predictable happens, as it does sometimes, although far less often than our paranoia might expect; Pacific Coast Guy is standing in the doorway of the corner shop, watching as morning turns into afternoon, summoning customers with his impatience. Gastón sees him at a point when crossing the road would have been too dramatic a gesture, born of fear, caution or a desire to snub. He opts for feigned indifference, which we know will fail miserably. He raises and lowers his eyebrows in greeting and tries to slip past, but Pacific Coast Guy bends down to stroke Kitten.

'What a handsome fellow!' he says. 'What breed is he?'

Gastón doesn't reply because he is speculating whether this change in attitude is all part of the act, a strategy to ease the tension and get him to let down his guard.

'Hey,' Pacific Coast Guy says, standing back up and changing the subject without waiting for Gastón's reply, 'don't you grow red potatoes?'

It must be a slow day in the shop, Gastón thinks – Pacific Coast Guy is bored and using any opportunity, including the appearance of Gastón, his supposed enemy, to blurt out things that gradually percolate in his mind between one customer and the next.

'Do you know it?' he goes on. 'Red potato – it's really small, you cook it with meat in a sauce; it's really tasty, and the potatoes from here don't taste of anything. Do you know how many kinds of potato there are in my homeland?' he asks. 'Over a hundred,' he replies, without even leaving time for a dramatic pause to form. 'Here you only get frying potatoes, cooking potatoes; these people know nothing about potatoes, it's just dreadful.'

Pacific Coast Guy has paid such vehement tribute to the potatoes from his homeland that now Gastón does, in fact, recall having grown them once, several years ago, at the request of a restaurant. Of course, he doesn't tell the owner of the corner shop this – he doesn't want to encourage the man's yearning for tubers – but for Pacific Coast Guy it's more than enough that Gastón is still there, that he's not walked off yet.

'Why don't you grow them and I'll sell them?' he says. 'Loads of my countrymen come here, and it's an expensive potato, even more than over there – we could sell it at any price we like, a kilo can cost three or four times as much as those bland local potatoes.'

The sudden leap from culinary wistfulness to business proposal makes Gastón relax a little, loosens the knot of tension; but this relief takes place inside his head, and he says nothing, doesn't even give an indication that he has heard Pacific Coast Guy's little speech, and his apparent indifference leads the man to pull at the knot once more, hard.

'You think you're better than everyone else, don't you?' he says, interpreting Gastón's silence as proof of his contempt. 'You think you're better because you don't know what someone like me has had to go through to get here. We don't all have the luxury of being good people, of having good feelings towards our neighbours – if only you could understand, but how on earth can you; it's just not possible.'

Now Gastón does try to say something, to refute this accusation, but it's too late; the shopkeeper interrupts him.

'Your dog's crapped outside my shop,' he says, and Gastón looks down at Kitten to check the bowel movement. 'You need to clean it up. Don't leave your shit outside my shop.'

Pacific Coast Guy goes back inside his shop. Gastón takes out a plastic bag and bends down to pick up the excrement, which is shot through with blood. Kitten flattens his ears against his head and his eyes fill with tears.

'It's OK,' Gastón says. 'Come on, let's go and find Max and Pol.'

52

He doesn't know if he hasn't seen him or is pretending not to have done. Gastón slips into the Far Eastern budget bazaar and watches the older man through the broken shop window. He is in the bar opposite, sitting at a table from where he can observe all the comings and goings out in the street, especially anyone entering or leaving the building that houses the restaurant and Max's home.

'You know him?' says Yu, from behind the counter.

Gastón and the dog have burst into the bazaar so dramatically that Yu immediately understands what's going on.

'Do you know who he is?' Yu insists, opening a notebook on the counter to take down the details, as if he were a reporter.

Gastón considers buying a hat and a pair of sunglasses to try and trick the older man, but rejects the idea as ridiculous as soon as he visualises it. He has nothing to hide; the one thing he must ensure is that he doesn't compromise Pol in any way. He must leave the bazaar, turn round and get out of there, get his phone and go home. It was reckless, Pol did warn him, but Gastón needed to check that the boy isn't experiencing an unjustified attack of paranoia. At least in this case, Gastón consoles himself (a fool's consolation), it seems that Pol was not exaggerating, and the older man is indeed determined to track him down.

'Do you know who he is?' Yu says again, puzzled by Gastón's silence, by his wary manner.

'I don't know,' Gastón says, not paying attention to what the Far Easterner is saying, preoccupied with plotting his escape route.

'You don't know?' Yu replies. 'What do you mean, you don't know?'

The Far Easterner walks over to where Gastón has stationed himself, close to the door, in what he thinks is a blind spot for the older man. Gastón says he's not sure, that he looks familiar, that he reminds him of someone, but that he could be wrong.

'He's been hanging around here for a couple of days now,' Yu says. 'He goes into the bar and he sits there by the window, keeping watch. Very suspicious. Look.'

He goes back over to the counter and picks up his notebook.

'Yesterday he arrived at nine forty-two,' the Far Easterner says. 'He stayed in the bar until eleven o eight. He walked up and down the street three times, talked to two people who came out of the building where the restaurant is that belongs to – what's your friend's name?'

'Max,' Gastón says.

'To Max,' Yu nods. 'Then he went back to the bar, until one forty.'

Gastón's first impulse, as he listens to the Far Easterner detail the older man's routine, is to correct his mistake, clear up the misunderstanding, do away with his suspicions, but he soon realises that the man's vigilance, besides being harmless (and a form of occupational therapy during the dead period in the bazaar), might be useful to him.

'You're right,' Gastón says, 'it's very suspicious. Can you let me know if anything strange happens?'

'Strange?' the Far Easterner says, making the corresponding phonetic effort.

Gastón says that he doesn't like how the man is loitering around Max's restaurant.

'How's your dog?' Yu asks suddenly, changing the subject, and Gastón notices that the Far Easterner is looking at Kitten with concern.

He follows the man's gaze and discovers why: the dog has spattered the floor tiles in the bazaar with blood, thick drops of the stuff that trickle down his hairy tail.

'Don't worry,' Yu says, 'I'll clean it up.'

The Far Easterner walks over to the counter, picks up a roll of kitchen paper and returns to where the dog is lying.

'What are you waiting for?' Yu asks.

'Nothing, I'm off,' Gastón replies, tugging hard at Kitten's lead to let him know they are going to have to walk fast, faster than he should really make the dog go.

'To put your friend to sleep, I mean,' the Far Easterner clarifies.

He is bending down, squatting really, waiting for the paper to soak up the blood; Gastón turns so that he is looking right at the man.

'I'm working on it,' he says, trying to justify himself, and grows embarrassed, as if, as well as giving explanations to the Far Easterner, he is giving them to himself, too, out loud, or to us, who do not share Gastón's selfish prevarication, either.

53

He has only just collected his phone from the Near Easterner's shop, when he gets a message: 'Hello, my friend,' we read; the sender, to Gastón's surprise, is listed in his contacts under the name of Ender (who – or what – is Ender?) and the message arrives not via the instant messaging app that everyone uses, but another one, which he wasn't even aware he had installed. 'Don't worry, this is secure, we can speak safely here.' Gastón starts to think that he really ought to get another phone, perhaps even another number, but then the explanation arrives: 'I'm from the phone shop.' On the screen we see the man typing for a few tiresome seconds, with pauses in between, perhaps so as to choose his words well, or perhaps it's just that one of the two of them has a bad connection.

'Sorry for saying that thing about porn, I didn't know what you were interested in. But you can't do these things this way, it's dangerous.' He explains that he's installed a firewall, some antivirus software, a private browser and an app that automatically erases your search history as you go. Gastón replies with a 'What do you want', which we aren't sure the Near Easterner knows to interpret as a threat. 'Relax, my friend, it's just so I can invite you. We've got a group, we meet up with other contactees, it's safe, there's no reason to worry.' 'I don't understand,' Gastón writes. 'Come along tonight,' the Near Easterner replies, 'you're in luck, we've got a meeting today. Here:' and Gastón is sent a time and an address. 'What is it?' he asks. 'It's what you were looking for,' we read on the screen. We wait for another message to arrive, but nothing. Gastón tries again, sending a solitary question mark. 'The Society of Friends of the Visitors from Space,' the Near Easterner writes. 'Join us.'

54

When the service door to the mansion opens, we see, beyond the cook, the father of the best footballer on Earth. He is drinking a herbal infusion from the Southern Cone, sitting at a long table, staring at his phone.

'Come in,' he says. 'I'll have them make you an infusion.'

Before Gastón can decline, or explain that he doesn't like the herbal infusions from the Southern Cone, or say that actually he would prefer a coffee, one of the maids bustling about in the kitchen hands him the receptacle. Another woman drags the sack of earth-covered potatoes from the same part of the Earth as the best footballer on Earth inside, while yet another asks her to leave a few out for her because she is about to make a stew for dinner.

'Have a seat,' the father of the best footballer on Earth says to Gastón in the firm tone of an order, as opposed to an invitation.

Gastón walks carefully over so as not to spill the infusion, and takes a sip of the scalding, bitter liquid.

'What do you think?' the father says as soon as Gastón has sat down.

'About what?' Gastón replies.

Another maid places a tray on the table containing biscuits, chocolates and a selection of confectionery.

'About what's going on with the kid,' the father says. 'Do you have children?'

Gastón says that he doesn't.

'Are you married?'

Gastón replies in the negative once again, and the father of the best footballer on Earth apologises for his lack of tact, says that it's fine, there's nothing to be ashamed of – he wouldn't have expected this sort of thing from a farmer, it used to be just hairdressers, theatre people, dressmakers, but not to worry, we live in different times now. Gastón doesn't even have time to think about correcting him, because the other man doesn't stop talking and now returns to the topic of his son's physical fitness, the pressures surrounding him (we hear him say), the management, the media, his teammates (and his family, Gastón would like to add, although he stays silent).

'Delicious, no?' the father says, indicating the receptacle containing the infusion.

Before Gastón can say anything, the father of the best footballer on Earth shouts to the maid to bring him another one and to please take care with the temperature of the water, because they always scald the leaves.

'Have you ruled out some kind of gastric problem?' Gastón asks, to say something, during the pause that follows as the other man takes a sip of his infusion.

'All gastric problems are here,' says the father, and he doesn't point at his stomach, his chest or his breastbone: he points at his head.

A different maid brings him another receptacle, and places a thermos of hot water next to it. The father of the best footballer on Earth waits for Gastón to complete the ceremony of pouring the hot liquid onto the leaves.

'And just as the most important part of the season's beginning,' he says.

The father gives a grumpy snort, bearing out the stereotype repeated a million times, that mawkish sentiment which tends to get called 'a fact of life': that children always disappoint their parents – even this child, even this father. Gastón thinks that he's referring to the final stage of the various championships, to the crucial game coming up in the next few days in the continental championship, but the father is talking about something else.

'Now's the time when all the sponsorship contracts are renewed for next year,' he explains.

He shakes his head, and then lowers it towards the screen of his phone, suddenly ignoring Gastón.

'You won't say anything, will you?' he asks.

'No, of course not,' Gastón replies, not really understanding what the secret is that has supposedly been revealed to him, and pushes his chair back in order to stand up.

'Relax,' the father says, 'enjoy your infusion; I've got a few small matters to clear up, but don't go just yet.'

'I have to go,' says Gastón, 'I've left my dog in the van.'

'Stay,' insists the father. 'Try these biscuits,' he orders, passing him one, 'they'll take you back to your childhood.'

The biscuit melts softly in Gastón's mouth, as if defying the laws of matter; it does not, however, take him back to his childhood (it makes him worry about the amount of butter it contains). If, as it seems, judging by this biscuit, the cooks in the mansion have a liberal approach when it comes to using butter and, by extension, oil, salt and garlic, this could be the explanation for the best footballer on Earth's gastric problems.

He glances up at the clock on the wall, calculating that he won't be able to get to his daily appointment with the sedatoress in time. The father of the best footballer on Earth is still engrossed in typing on his phone; Gastón sees his chance and takes his own phone from his trouser pocket. 'I'm sorry,' he writes, 'it's got a little late here. We're not going to get there in time. See you tomorrow?' The messages are delivered right away, and we watch the sedatoress typing away, wherever she is. 'I'm already on my way . . . Do you know how to give an injection?' Gastón says that he does. 'I thought as much,' the sedatoress replies, sending the crying-with-laughter emoji. 'I'll leave the dose in the mailbox by the gate,' we read, 'just don't inject yourself, you druggie.'

55

The address the Near Easterner has sent him is the basement of a bar Gastón knows well; it's a place that usually hosts book launches, poetry readings, literary discussion groups and oratory clubs, one of the neighbourhood's more traditional spots, and this – the fact that it's not secret – he finds strange. The predictable, in this case, does not apply, and he therefore doesn't know what to expect. He keeps watch over the hustle and bustle of the street from over the road, so he can get an idea about the kind of people who have responded to the meeting that has been called, and calculate how many are attending. He believes himself protected by the darkness, by the gloom given off by the grubby street-lamps, by the absence of Kitten, whom he has left at home, happily sleeping his morphine-induced sleep. In a way, it's as if Gastón believes that people do not recognise him without his dog, without this appendage at the end of a lead. He is discovered, though; by Ender, by chance, when he bumps into him as he rounds the corner.

'It's great that you've come along,' the man says. 'It's just over there,' he adds, nodding towards the bar opposite.

The Near Easterner doesn't give him a chance to react and Gastón is practically dragged over by the momentum of the man's harmless prattle, which does away with any sense of intrigue or conspiracy.

'You have to pay to get in,' he says, 'but since it's your first time I'll talk to the organisers so they won't charge you.'

Gastón replies that he can't stay for long, an excuse he has thought up before getting here in case he has to leave in a hurry. He tells him about the dog's ill health and says that he ought to get back sooner rather than later, that he doesn't like leaving the animal on his own, and sedated on top of that (although this last thing, naturally, he doesn't say out loud, just thinks it).

They enter the bar and walk through it and down the stairs leading to the event space and the toilets. It's an old-fashioned place, one of those that seems to have been there for ever, where the owner keeps bar and the employees are all Southern Coners, the tables are made of iron and marble, a football flag is hanging above the bar (which lets us know that this is where a group of fans of the city team gets together to watch matches), and a sign saying, 'For sale due to retirement', which Gastón knows conceals the fact of the owner's arthritis.

Downstairs, a woman is collecting the entrance fee and Ender keeps his promise. He manages to get in for free, too, by bringing someone new (a reward for recruiting people).

'We have to wait for the leader,' the Near Easterner says. 'Sometimes he's a little late. Come on, I'll introduce you to everyone.'

He takes him over to a woman who says she is a secretary at the consulate of one of the ex-Colonies of the Far West; a stout man with a pockmarked face (Ender whispers that he is an important businessman, the owner of a yoghurt factory); to a very young couple who Gastón thinks he recognises as regulars at Max's restaurant; and an old man who introduces himself as a local councillor. They are all chatting noisily about the 'last few messages received' and 'the instructions sent by the visitors from space', as the Near Easterner explains to him.

Gastón grows distracted for two good reasons: firstly, because this all sounds like a childish fantasy to him, and secondly, because he is wondering how he can get to talk to the old man, the councillor, about applying for planning permission for the land his market garden is on. He can't quite think clearly in the midst of all the hubbub, and before he can make up his mind about anything, Ender nudges him with his elbow to get his attention.

'We're starting,' he informs Gastón.

In the basement of the bar, followed by a small group he seems to be controlling with a dog lead, the leader of the society has just appeared. We can't see him very clearly, because people are crowding round him; Gastón moves his head to help us identify him, to try and get a look at his face. He looks to him like an old teacher from Pol's primary school, who was thrown out years ago for not following the curriculum and instead indoctrinating the students with the most outlandish theories. Gastón knows he must take advantage of the commotion to escape; he tells Ender he is going to the toilet and slips out of the room without anyone noticing.

It's a single toilet, absolutely tiny, where you can wash your hands while still sitting on the loo. Gastón bolts the door, puts the lid down, takes a seat and tries to listen, but all he is able to catch from the multiple conversations are random, scattered phrases, odd words that seem like they come straight out of fiction: 'expedition members', 'reconnaissance mission', 'contactees', 'the leader of the Peninsular mission'. He tries to remember exactly where the bathroom is located, where the stairs are, what can be seen from the event space; he ought to have just slipped out for good instead of hiding in the toilet. If Gastón were a more calculating man, more distrustful, more paranoid, he wouldn't have found himself in this situation; but the best adventures happen to the people who are least prepared for them, to average guys who have no reason to imagine they might end up locked in a bathroom while outside a meeting held by people contacted by an alien civilisation is taking place.

Outside the bathroom there is a silence which (we can easily guess) precedes a speech. Gastón calculates that if the speaker is facing the audience, he will have his back to the toilet, to the stairs. He feels the tingling in his stiff legs and concludes that he cannot allow himself to be overcome by indecision, as he will end up paralysed; he must take advantage of the speech starting, when everyone there will be paying attention, concentrating on the leader; he has to get out of there immediately. He stands up, stealthily unbolts the door, pushes it half open, walks across the passageway like the shadow of a cat and reaches the stairs.

56

The Society of Friends of the Visitors from Space has a blog, which hasn't been updated for several years, but which no one has bothered to take down, either. Lying in his bed in the darkness, Gastón confirms the identity of the old teacher from Pol's school in the photos of the society's meetings, looking for all the world like the society pages of a newspaper, and the glare from the screen makes us blink to protect our retinas; for a secret group of conspiracy theorists they don't exactly keep quiet about their initiatives. Going over the posts, we read that the ex-teacher even stood for mayor of the city on a platform against the universal fascism that proposed the unconditional surrender of papers for everyone, reptiles, arthropods and Greys.

Before he can drop off, Gastón gets a message from Ender: 'Why didn't you stay? They made me pay the entrance fee thanks to you.' His first impulse is to ignore it, but he soon reconsiders. 'Sorry,' he writes, 'it was an emergency, a friend of mine was in trouble' (a lie). He pauses so that he can put together the following lines in his head, feigning the naturalness he needs to soften his request. 'Can you do me a favour?' he types. 'You know the councillor who . . . ' He stops, goes back and deletes everything he's written. 'Don't worry,' he types, 'I'll come by the shop tomorrow and give you the money – apologies, it was an emergency.' Gastón sends the message, switches off his phone, says good night to Kitten, who he had to carry from the living room to his little bed next to Gastón's, and closes his eyes to let us know that that's quite enough for today, that he is exhausted (are we aware of everything that's happened in one day?), that this story will continue tomorrow – that is, on the next page.

57

Gastón is in the market garden when he receives the meme, taking a break to give his back a rest; he has been pulling up elongated onions from the earth and stacking them in the crates he uses for deliveries. On the phone's screen, we can see Yu typing, behind the counter in his bazaar we imagine, taking advantage of the lack of customers first thing in the morning. 'Hahahahahaha,' the new message says, 'hahahahahahahaha.'

'What is it?' Gastón replies, as he hasn't downloaded the image with the joke (we can just about see that it's a photo with that text in capital letters at the top and bottom which characterises memes); he waits for the reply, wiping the sweat from his brow and calculating that he has less than an hour's work to finish harvesting the elongated onions from this plot.

Yu types for a long time. He takes so long that we start to doubt his syntactic and narrative capabilities, and when at last a message does come through we see that it's a string of emojis. Gastón is not going to reply; he doesn't want to give any sign of approval, he must prevent the Far Easterner from pestering him from now on with his humorous correspondence. He glances over towards the tool shed, where Kitten is lying; he locks the screen and puts his phone away, pulls his gloves back on, picks up the hoe and prepares to continue loosening the earth around the elongated onions. Before he goes back to this task, however, two of his tens of thousands of millions of neurons form a synapse to inform him of what he has only glimpsed out of the corner of his eye, something he has barely noticed and which could have some significance. One of the emojis. A little cartoon alien; the cute, inoffensive symbol of a little grey humanoid, to be precise.

He drops the hoe, takes off his gloves and gets his phone out again. He downloads the image of what we thought was a meme: it's a photo of the older man. 'THREE PM', we read at the top of the picture. And at the bottom: 'ENTRANCE TO THE HISTORIC PARK'.

We look carefully at the series of emojis, trying to decipher the message. There are some that look significant, like an eye, which we suppose must mean that Yu saw or discovered something; a sequence of pieces of paper and padlocks, which could be referring to archived documents or, more likely, secret information; and the aforementioned little grey man. But we've had to extract this from among dozens of little smiling or weeping faces, of animals (dogs, cats, monkeys, octopuses, unicorns, chickens), flowers, fruit (apples, straw-berries, kiwis, melons, watermelons), footballs, aeroplanes, teddy bears and, as if that weren't enough, various hearts in different colours (red, green, blue, yellow). Gastón gives a snort and the resulting spray of spittle is proof that the situation is exasperating him, that he would rather not start playing at spy films with the Far Easterner; then he sighs and shakes his head, conditioned by acting stereotypes, trying to justify himself, to express that there is nothing for it, as if someone were watching him, as if he owed us an explanation.

58

Gastón follows the councillor from reception through to a meeting room, twenty minutes later than the arranged time. He is impatient, less so because of the wait, which was predictable in the bureaucratic toing and froing any morning contains, and more because he has left Kitten on his own back in the market garden. The councillor strides down the corridors of the local government headquarters at a hectic pace, as if feigning busyness, or perhaps he really is very busy; Gastón doubts it, for if this were the case the man wouldn't have been able to see him so quickly, right after Ender called him to request the meeting.

In the basement of the bar, the councillor looked older to us than he actually is, a sixty-something closer to sixty than to seventy. From his simple way of dressing – like any old office worker – one might surmise that today there are no official activities in his diary, or none that he is responsible for, at least. The meeting room isn't ostentatious, either; the only thing distinguishing it from any of the other rooms where bureaucrats, executives, businesspeople or liberal professionals meet is that, in one corner, there is a municipal flag (and quite a shabby one at that).

Gastón closes the glass door behind him, and the councillor, with an excitement he can barely conceal – or, rather, that he fails to conceal – holds up his phone, triumphant.

'Look, Gastón – I've got a new message,' he says, 'it came early this morning.'

He sits down at the head of the table as his fingers tap away at the screen of his phone. Gastón takes a seat in the chair next to his, even though the councillor has not invited him to do so; these are the customs and habits of the city, this absence of courtesy, these brusque codes which now, after so many years, he accepts automatically, without question.

'Listen,' the councillor says, and places the phone on the table, in front of Gastón.

Before the sound comes on, we see that it's a voice message received via the instant messaging app. Then we hear a metallic sound, a voice that's been distorted using one of those programmes they use on TV to hide the identity of witnesses or of people reporting a crime, although, in this case, the distortion is so extreme that it makes most of the message completely unintelligible. 'Violence', we make out, or perhaps it says 'non-violence'; 'rebellion', 'mission', 'expedition'; for some reason the words ending in '-ion' are the easiest to make out with this level of distortion. To make matters worse, the message is constantly broken up by an interference that reminds us of previous eras, archaic forms of communication like radios or portable transmitters.

'It's long,' the councillor says, picking up the phone and pausing the message, 'nearly eight minutes. Did you receive anything last night?'

He closes the messaging app and puts his phone away quickly, so that he can concentrate on Gastón's answer.

'I haven't received any messages yet,' Gastón replies.

The councillor smiles because he has reason to believe that he is one of the few chosen ones and that, within the hierarchy of the group of contactees, Gastón is in a position of inferiority. He could act arrogantly, but opts instead for being patronising; touching him lightly on the arm, he tells Gastón that if they want to contact him then they will, and if not, then it doesn't matter, that each person in the group has a different task in the mission and that all the tasks are important. 'Transcendental' is the word he chooses to underline this supposed importance. When he has finished consoling Gastón, a silence forms like a full stop and a new paragraph, to change the subject, a silence that takes the place of the question the councillor ought to ask and does not, an invitation for Gastón to explain the reason for his visit, which forces Gastón to take the initiative.

Rather than laying out his query directly, Gastón begins to talk about Max's restaurant, about the market garden, about growing the peppers Max used to use, to make salsa for the nachos and stews from his homeland, about how they've been friends for thirty years.

'I've only agreed to see you because Ender told me you were from the group,' the councillor says, cutting in, suddenly fearing, as he listens to this quaint tale filled with local colour, that there has been a misunderstanding.

Gastón says yes, yes, yes, a hurried, ambiguous yes which he hopes serves to reassure the councillor, so that he can at least have the chance to outline his problem to the man. The truth is that persuading Ender to help him cost him the price of two tickets to the event with the contactees – Ender's ticket and Gastón's – to assuage the Near Easterner, who was accusing Gastón of having put him in a really difficult position by running off.

'My plan,' Gastón says, after beating around the bush for a while, 'is to build a property in the market garden.'

'You won't get planning permission for a change of use,' the councillor says, in a bored voice, without waiting for Gastón to finish explaining. 'There's a ban on that until further notice. Until the government changes – you know how it works.'

Another silence, although this time it sounds like a definitive full stop, a new chapter, something that might entail a disappointment, a fresh obstacle to be overcome. Gastón sits and looks carefully at the councillor, trying to weigh up whether the man's 'no' is genuine, or if it might be a strategy to increase the value of his involvement. Should Gastón ask him, innocently, if there's anything that can be done, an exception that can be made, some way of getting around the ban? He hesitates for five, ten, fifteen seconds, time that the councillor uses to activate his common sense – so similar, at times, to telepathy.

'I don't know how these things are resolved where you come from, sir,' he says, coldly, folding his arms, 'but here we obey the law. I must request that you do not say anything that might force me to draw up a formal charge of attempted bribery.'

Of all the reasons to be offended by what the councillor has just said, the thing that most wounds Gastón is the shift from a friendly tone to a more formal one, a transition that symbolises the loss of trust and familiarity, a downgrading that aims to humiliate him. Gastón pushes back his chair, stands up and, using the councillor's warning as an excuse, does not even open his mouth to say goodbye.

59

Yu is hidden in the middle of a group of Far Eastern tourists, his head bent over his phone, and Gastón doesn't know if it's a joke or if he's taking this spy game stuff literally. He is wearing a hat and dark glasses, chosen at random from the budget bazaar, we imagine, as they don't match either each other or the rest of his attire. Gastón stops a few feet away from the entrance to the Historic Park; Kitten senses the tension on his lead slackening and immediately flops down on the flowery pavement tiles.

The Far Easterner doesn't raise his head, engrossed in his phone, or pretending to be; we can't tell from this distance. Gastón waits for the other man to notice him and react, as the tourists walk past, dodging the dog's bulk as the animal blocks the path.

'Look up,' Gastón writes on his phone, and sends the message; he doesn't want to approach the group of tourists, not out of caution, or fear, but rather to avoid humouring the Far Easterner, avoid encouraging his childish cloak-and-dagger act. But Yu ignores him; instead of putting down his phone and looking around for Gastón, he replies with an emoji, or rather two: two men running, as if one is chasing after the other. The Far Easterner steps out from among the group of Far Eastern tourists and starts striding briskly down the street that runs along the side of the park. Gastón sighs, gives Kitten's lead a tug to let him know it's time to get up, and begins the pursuit.

They round the park's perimeter wall, a series of overlapping stones with a primitive sort of look, which supposedly serves as the border between the past and the present. We see the Far Easterner's back some way off, dodging tourists as they make use of the public wifi to prove to the world they exist, via their phones. Where is the Far Easterner going? What is he up to? The flow of tourists diminishes the further away they get from the entrance to the park; he is taking him somewhere off the beaten track where they'll be able to speak without anyone seeing them, Gastón reckons, as he thinks, somewhat flustered from the effort of keeping up the pace of the chase, that all this clowning around had better be in aid of something serious.

When they reach the western edge of the park, Yu turns west, going against the rotation of the Earth, and dives down the dirt track that leads, Gastón realises, to the lookout point. Finally, the Far Easterner stops and sits down on one of the benches where the tourists eat their snacks and climb up to take panoramic photos of the city.

Still at a distance, as he approaches and sees the Far Easterner with his hands in his jacket pockets, his eyes hidden behind the dark glasses and his face half in shadow under the hat, Gastón thinks that he could have sworn he'd seen this scene before, dozens of times, in the cinema or on TV. All around them, the tourists are chatting, some in languages we understand, with strange accents, and some in others we don't know. It's not a place to hide, as we anticipated, but it is a place to try and go unnoticed.

'He's still awake,' Yu says, looking at Kitten, when Gastón sits down next to him.

Kitten lies down at Gastón's feet as his owner breathes heavily to try and get his breath back. The Far Easterner leans forwards and strokes the dog's head.

'You're a bad friend,' he tells Gastón.

Before Gastón can say a word (if, that is, he was planning on setting out some argument in his defence), Yu speaks again.

'Who is he?'

'Who?' Gastón replies.

'Do you know who he is?' Yu says.

'Who?' Gastón says again, not because he doesn't know who the Far Easterner is talking about, but as a ploy, to play for time, so that the Far Easterner will explain his suspicions.

'You've seen what's happening,' Yu says. 'People who don't want us here. First they smash the windows in our shops and graffiti the walls, then there are thefts, threats.'

From what we hear Yu explain, it looks – or rather, sounds – like the Far Easterners are organising and have sought legal advice, after the police took the view that the attacks they experienced were a case of street vandalism with no identifiable source. Up until now, one of the clues they have followed, the most relevant, in fact, is that of the older man.

'We've spoken to him,' the Far Easterner says.

He pauses dramatically, or perhaps just in order to see if there is any reaction from Gastón.

'He told us he's here for Max's son,' the Far Easterner says, 'but we don't believe him; when we leant on him he started talking about bacteria: he says they're doing research into extraterrestrial life but that he can't explain it because it's top secret information, a load of nonsense, and I want you to tell me what's going on. You know what's going on.'

The Far Easterner removes his dark glasses and tries to meet Gastón's gaze, as if calculating whether or not he can trust him. Despite his sense of shame at benefitting from this misunderstanding, Gastón recognises how convenient it is for him, just at this moment. He looks around, confirming that this encounter will be recorded in dozens of tourist photos, although the likelihood that one of these images ends up giving them away when it is posted on social media is minimal. He stretches out his legs so that he can get his phone from his pocket, unlocks the screen and searches through the apps until he finds a phone number in his contacts. The lawyer from the country.

'I can tell you who's behind all this,' Gastón says, showing him the information on the screen, 'but you've got to help me, too.'

Before he copies down the number into his own phone, the Far Easterner wants to know the price.

'Don't take your eyes off him,' Gastón replies. 'I'll find you when I need something.'

60

'If Martians were going to invade the Earth, how would they do it?' the sedatoress asks.

They're leaning against the carob tree, side by side, almost touching, almost shoulder to shoulder, watching how, in front of them, Kitten peacefully sleeps his morphine sleep. They are on their third beer and creating a small mound of pistachio shells.

'Martians?' Gastón replies. 'There's no life on Mars.'

'Well, Venutians, then, or people from the moons of Jupiter,' the sedatoress says; 'wherever!'

A breeze softly stirs the branches of the tree and a carob pod, still green, comes loose and drops onto the dog's back, without disturbing him. The sedatoress takes a long drink of her beer, crushes the can in her right hand and sighs contentedly. She is a good drinker, we realise, one of those upon whom alcohol has a calming effect, making her more susceptible to glimpsing the continuum of time, the fact that nothing matters if it is situated in the right dimension – millions of years, for instance. The subject of alien life does not really interest her, but it looks like – it sounds like, based on what we can hear – ever since Gastón mentioned it she has been reading all kinds of theories on the internet, perhaps out of curiosity, perhaps so that she has something to talk about while she gives the dog his morphine.

Gastón describes the typical scene we are accustomed to seeing in fiction: spaceships, alien robots, weapons of mass destruction that use unfamiliar technology, an interplanetary war, the destruction of the Earth, our own extinction.

'But why would they destroy it,' the sedatoress replies, 'if what they want is to make use of our natural resources, to take over the Earth and exploit it like a colony?'

The sedatoress explains that, since they are a superior civilisation, the extraterrestrials would have a long-term approach, dedicating thousands of years to get to know the Earth and adapt to it; that they would make themselves pass as Earthlings and hide their evolutionary differences, although it would be hard for them to keep their superior intelligence secret; they would form a nomadic people, rootless, migrant, and gradually spread out across the planet this way.

'Maybe we're the ariens,' she concludes, caricaturing the pronunciation of the L in the word 'alien', turning it into the R that distinguishes the stereotypical pronunciation the Far Easterners are expected to use when speaking the colonising language.

They both laugh heartily.

'I like this place,' the sedatoress says, looking around the market garden; 'I'd settle for this, I'd set my colony up here.'

The truth is that now, halfway through harvesting, the market garden is not a particularly pretty place (plots with the earth turned over where before there were plants), but the sedatoress isn't talking about the view; she's talking about the peace, about the temperature, the silence, the wind, the smell of the earth. Gastón stares at her openly; he is a worse drinker than she is, and might be about to start to venture interpretations, to decipher supposed double meanings, to believe that the spider vein on the sedatoress's right cheek is a sign of something, the key to a riddle or a secret.

'Are you coming on to me?' Gastón says, half joking, half serious, the way that reckless words are always spoken.

'Sorry,' the sedatoress replies, 'we're not allowed to mate with the natives.'

Gastón moves his body closer to the sedatoress and gives her a little shove with his shoulder as he rocks with laughter.

'I will let you get me another beer, though,' the sedatoress says.

61

An urgent phone call from Max, asking him to go to the pharmacy, as Gastón is turning over the soil in the plot where the elongated onions have been growing. Something they ate was off, he explains, and all three of them – Pol, Max and his father – have diarrhoea, a slight fever and aching muscles, and are vomiting. Gastón is about to apologise, but he realises Max isn't even aware that it was he, Gastón, who put the food he thought was still all right into the freezer. Max asks him to put the bag with the medicine into the building's mailbox and let him know once he's done so. He then hangs up, without giving Gastón time to respond or remind him that he has a set of keys.

Gastón cleans the screen of his phone, which has got covered in earth, by rubbing it on his trousers. He takes off his gloves and makes a call.

'I need you to distract him,' he says, with no greeting or preamble.

'What's going on?' the Far Easterner replies.

'I've got to go and see Max, and I don't want the older man to see me,' Gastón says.

'He's in the bar,' Yu says, 'same as always.'

'In twenty minutes,' Gastón says, and hangs up.

He walks over to the tool shed to check he still has carob flour. There is enough for a two-day treatment for the three of them. He picks up the plastic bag, puts it inside another bag, a canvas one, and explains to Kitten that it's best if he doesn't come, because he has to be quick. He fills the dog's bowl with fresh water and places a handful of meat-flavoured treats near the animal, who watches him from his little bed.

'I won't be long,' Gastón says, and heads up the path leading to the garden gate.

62

He looks over at the street corner opposite – the one where Yu's bazaar is – and over at the bar across the road, but can't see the older man. It seems the Far Easterner can be trusted. Gastón hurries over to the restaurant and presses the switch by the entrance that opens the shutters. Inside, Max's father is leaning against the bar, staring at his phone.

'Where are Max and Pol?' Gastón asks, when he sees that no one else is in there.

'Upstairs,' Max's father replies. 'Do you want a beer?'

'It's ten thirty in the morning,' Gastón says.

'Seriously?' Max's father replies, walking over to the fridge. 'You want one or not?'

Gastón says that he doesn't.

'Sit down,' he tells Max's father. 'I need to talk to you.'

They take a seat at the bar, Max's father on the barman's side, with his bottle of beer and a plate of nachos in front of him, Gastón on the customers' side, with a Kitten-shaped space at his feet, a space the dog ought to be curled up in, as he always is.

'Did you know Max was bankrupt?' Max's father asks.

'What?' Gastón says, surprised.

'All that useless boy's got are debts,' Max's father says. 'Does he not owe you money?'

It isn't possible for Max to owe him a thing, Gastón thinks, given that money has not existed between the two of them for years. Gastón would grow the peppers and in exchange he got food and beer; their initial client–supplier relationship didn't last long, hardly any time at all, just until the day when the rules of etiquette from Max's homeland prevented him from charging Gastón for what he ate and drank in the restaurant, and then Gastón, in return, refused to let Max pay for his next order.

There is no need, however, for Gastón to tell any of this to Max's father, who is already explaining that his plan was to pass through the city to cash out, to recoup the return he is owed from his investment (these are the words he uses, even though we might not like them); that his bank accounts back home have been frozen, that he was counting on Max paying him back this money and is now trapped.

'He's squandered my assets,' Pol's grandfather says, accusing his son with the very same phrase we predicted a few chapters ago.

We watch him take a long drink of his beer, place the bottle back down on the bar decisively, tut loudly, and give a snort.

'I always knew it,' Max's father says. 'He's not to be counted on. And now he's going to run away like a little boy and leave me in the lurch.'

'I'm going to go up and see them,' Gastón says, knowing from experience that it's better to cut Max's father off now than to have to put up with his hate-filled spiel, the superiority he assumes for having been born earlier, in a time of heroism and virile certainties, and he stands up, pushing back his seat.

'Listen,' Max's father says.

Gastón pauses in his escape.

'Can you lend me some money?'

Max's father explains that he needs to get to a place where he has several bank accounts that haven't been located yet, one of the tax havens in the Central West. From there, he says, he can make an anonymous transfer, and he is even prepared to pay Gastón a generous amount of interest. This sounds to Gastón like those fraudulent emails we all receive so often, the widow who can't claim her inheritance or the prince from the South who needs associates to extract a fortune from his kingdom.

How much will it cost to help Max's father? Gastón wonders, although in fact, what really interests him is knowing how much he would have to give the man to make him disappear. He does a quick sum in his head, adding up travel costs and hotel and food in some city a few hours away, we imagine, any one of those secret enclaves that feature on maps purely out of an embarrassed desire to be true to geography.

'How much?' Gastón asks.

Max's father picks up a serviette and writes down a figure. It's a little higher than what Gastón had calculated.

'In cash,' Max's father specifies, 'in small notes.'

Suddenly it seems as if we're in a mafia story: the empty restaurant, dimly lit, and this pompous old man, drinking beer at breakfast time and giving instructions to Gastón as if he were shaking him down for protection money or a kidnap ransom.

Gastón picks up the serviette and puts it in his trouser pocket, even though he has memorised the figure, so that

Max's father understands that he will consider the request, without needing to give him an answer right away. Max's father asks for the medicine, tells him he is sick of being stuck in the toilet, and that this is why he came down to the restaurant, so as not to have to fight with Max and Pol for the throne. Gastón replies that what he has brought is a natural remedy, which needs preparing. Max's father snorts again, louder this time.

63

There's no answer, and he has to use the key he has on the same ring as the ones for the restaurant. When he pushes the door, something is stopping him from opening it; he imagines that Pol or Max has stationed himself there to defend the fortress from attack.

'It's me, Gastón,' he whispers, going along with the paranoia and the plotting, through force of habit or imitation, in order to respect the rules of the genre.

He puts his ear up to the crack but can hear nothing. He pushes again, cautiously at first, then hard, but only manages to get the door half open. He turns sideways and sucks in his stomach to slip in, and we see that the thing blocking the door is a pile of boxes. There are more, in the hallway and the passage that leads to the living room.

'What's going on?' Gastón asks, standing in the living room doorway after he's dodged the obstacles.

The blinds are closed and all the lights are on, as if it were eleven o'clock at night, not in the morning. Pol is lying on the sofa, faithfully playing the part of a sick man, buried under several layers of blankets despite the fact that it's a warm day; Max is wandering around the apartment sorting papers, putting some into boxes, others into great big black plastic sacks, reinforced ones, the ones he used to use in the restaurant for rubbish (judging by the speed at which he is carrying out this procedure, it doesn't seem like the criteria are particularly strict).

'Did you see my boss down there?' Pol asks in reply. 'Is he still watching the exit?'

It is revealing that Pol describes the door of the building as the exit and not the entrance. The exit: the escape route. Gastón decides to conceal his alliance with the Far Easterner, like an overprotective father who prefers to keep his child innocent of his ploys.

'Did you bring the medicine?' Max asks.

There are stacks of things on the dining room table, clothes piled up in the corners, pictures that have been taken off the wall and are now leaning against it. It smells of sweaty bed sheets, of damp, of ancient dust, the scent things give off after having been forgotten, of time stirred up.

'What's going on?' Gastón says again.

'I need to know if he's still there,' Pol replies.

'Do you need anything?' Max asks Gastón. 'Take whatever you want.'

Gastón goes over to Max, he has to pursue him, stand in his way, force him to stop.

'What's going on?' he asks once more, although he already knows what's going on (we can hear the flow of his thoughts, or rather of his fears), but he believes he is owed an explanation.

Max puts his right hand on Gastón's shoulder so he doesn't have to look him in the eye.

'We're going home,' he says; 'the day after tomorrow. We've got flights booked. I'm going to talk to the people who bought the restaurant, the North Easterners or whoever they are,' he goes on, without giving Gastón time to ask where he supposes home is. 'They can keep everything in it, see what they can make use of, and anything else they can throw away. I won't have time to think about all that.'

'When did you decide to leave?' Gastón asks, preferring to use the verb he feels is appropriate here, rather than 'go back'.

'I've been thinking about it for a while,' Max says. 'The restaurant hasn't been going well for a long time.'

'What?' Gastón says, with no idea how to react and thinking that he is owed a better explanation.

Max says that the city is crawling with restaurants from his homeland, and as if that weren't enough, everyone is doing nachos and avocado salsa now, even the Far Eastern bars.

'But where are you going to go?' Gastón asks.

'To my mum's, at first,' Max says. 'She needs us, she's older now, she shouldn't be on her own.'

'She's got her other children and her grandkids,' Gastón replies, clinging to denial.

'It's your fault,' Max says. 'You scared her with your messages – she was the one who convinced me to go home.'

'You didn't tell me,' Gastón says.

'You sound like an old married couple,' Pol says, watching them from the sofa.

We could swear that Max is thinking the same thing that's going through Gastón's mind, as they both look at Pol, shivering under his blankets and giving off a subtle but tenacious pong (he can't have showered for days, following Max's example): that if this were the case, then they would have failed to properly bring up the son they raised together.

'I thought you wanted us to open a restaurant in the market garden,' Gastón says, ignoring Pol.

'What?' Max replies.

'You were talking the other day about getting planning permission for the land,' Gastón says. 'I thought we could build a new place out there.'

'I said that because Biel called me,' Max replies.

'Who?' Gastón says.

'He told me you'd been to the estate agent's,' Max says, 'saying you wanted to buy a premises, and he said I should convince you to apply for planning permission to build on the land, because the market's buoyant at the moment and now would be the time to do it and to sell.'

'Biel's a fraud,' Pol says.

'I kept telling you,' Max says to Gastón, adamant, not looking at Pol, 'but you never listened. You've got to think about your retirement.'

'Biel didn't tell me he'd spoken to you,' Gastón says.

'Like a married couple who don't talk to each other,' Pol says.

64

He hurries down the stairs, and with each step his sense of foreboding increases. If we were to be strictly accurate, we would say that, more than foreboding, it is a conclusion, the consequence of tying up loose ends, of threading together the logic of the story. He doesn't have to wait to confirm it; down in the hall, the restaurant's letter box is overflowing with post. Gastón pushes his fingertips in through the slit and pulls out the first few envelopes he can reach: unpaid bills, repossession orders, court summons, threats from suppliers.

Max is going to flee the city, now that he can. He's going to escape from the present, which is threatening him, to the past. Gastón stops before opening the door to the street. He takes his phone from his pocket and makes a call.

'I'm leaving,' he says, 'I need you to cover my back.'

'Hang on,' the Far Easterner says, 'I've got customers – give me five minutes. I'll give you a missed call.'

65

He opens the gate to the market garden, closes it behind him and does the padlock up again, calculating how much it is that Max owes, whether he can convince his friend to let himself be helped, to not run away, to stay. He walks down the path that leads to the tool shed, and when he's five yards or so away he realises: Kitten isn't breathing. He's lying on his little bed, just as Gastón left him a couple of hours ago, in the same position, on his right side, his legs drawn in, curled up, his eyes closed, the meat-flavoured treats intact a few feet from his muzzle.

Gastón doesn't think what we, so eager to assign meaning to everything, might venture to guess: that Kitten has chosen this moment to die, that he has expired now purely to save Gastón from the pain of watching him go, has chosen to speed up the process now that Max and Pol are leaving, and that all of this represents the end of an era. We'd like to believe that this is the case, to make a case for the dog's awareness, even for a certain paranormal sense, but let's not deceive ourselves – these are romantic speculations we use to console ourselves. Gastón's first impulse, meanwhile, is to blame himself: he has failed his pet, he should have been there by his side at the end. He sits down on the ground by the tool shed, next to Kitten, next to the animal's still-warm body, and starts to stroke his head and his back.

We are going to leave them alone; we have no right to be there now, we're going to stick our noses in somewhere else; we'll walk over to the carob tree, our backs to Gastón and to Kitten's body, and we'll stay there for a while, looking down at the city, not turning round, displaying a sense of shame, of decency, and we'll prove that, even when writing fiction, there is a moral and an ethical framework that must be respected.

66

During each break he takes to give his shoulder a rest, he checks his phone. He plans to keep on digging for as long as the roots of the carob tree let him, the deeper the better, and in any case, he's killing time as he waits for Max and Pol to get back to him. He doesn't want to bury Kitten alone – it has to be done as a family, that's what the dog would have wanted. But Max and Pol have ignored all his calls, or not seen them. In the end Gastón sent them a message telling them to get in touch urgently. And in the meantime, he continues to strike the earth with his spade, rhythmically, resolutely, but without anger, without rage, just resigned.

When at last he feels his phone buzzing in his pocket, he answers it without looking at the screen.

'Gastón?' we hear a woman's voice say, before explaining, all in a rush and with an accent from the Southern Cone, that it's his cousin, or rather his cousin's wife, the cousin who is Gastón's father's sister's son, and telling him not to hang up as it's very important he hears her out.

Gastón mutters a hello and tells her that it's really not a good time.

'There's no time to lose,' the woman says, mentioning the urgency of the situation yet again.

'What is it?' Gastón asks, managing despite the circumstances to reason that before he hangs up and blocks this cousin's number, it wouldn't be a bad idea to find out what she wants.

The woman tells him that two of her nephews (also Gastón's nephews), that is, the sons of one of her husband's brothers (or, just so we're clear, sons of one of Gastón's cousins), have lodged an appeal against Gastón to dispossess him of the properties he inherited from his father.

'Thanks for informing me,' Gastón interrupts her. 'I'll speak to a lawyer.'

'No, you don't get it,' the cousin says. 'it sounds as if you've forgotten what things are like here.'

The accusation offends Gastón, as do all those phrases used by those who stay behind to express their resentment and ill will towards those who leave, as if remaining in the same place conferred upon them some sort of superiority. Gastón recalls his relatives' tired old refrains on the rare occasions he's had contact with them since he left: 'Well, it's easy for you to say that because you don't live here anymore'; 'Things aren't like they used to be'; 'You've got to be here to realise that. . . '; and 'Leaving's the easy option'.

'Gastón?' the cousin asks, fearing she's been hung up on.

'Yep,' Gastón replies, already beginning to calculate how serious this threat is.

'They paid off the judge,' the cousin tells him. 'They made it look as if you'd been notified so you wouldn't find out – if you don't come to the hearing then you'll receive a default judgment and they'll win. I'm sending you the documents now, by text.'

'I have to hang up now,' Gastón says, doubly unsettled: by what he's just been told, and because he fears that Max or Pol might be calling him back at this very moment.

'I'll send you the documents,' the cousin says.

'Thank you,' Gastón replies.

'Hey,' the cousin says, before he can hang up, 'don't you forget it was me who told you all this, eh? Everyone in the family knew and no one said a word to you.'

67

Gastón walks back up the path that leads to the gate, wanting it to be Pol and Max; but his hope that they've come without letting him know first, slipping past the older man's surveillance or facing him down, when they saw how insistently Gastón has been calling them and sensed the urgency of the situation – this hope vanishes when he recognises the Near Easterner and the councillor waiting on the other side of the gate.

'I can't do this now,' Gastón says, his right hand closing around the bunch of keys hanging from the belt loop of his trousers to hide them. 'I'm busy.'

'It's urgent,' Ender replies.

'We've come because this can't be discussed over the phone,' the councillor says. 'We can't expose ourselves like that.'

Before Gastón is able to finish speculating (that perhaps this is the continuation of the chat he had with the councillor at the local government headquarters, the part where the councillor tells him there is a way to sort these things out), the Near Easterner and the councillor fall over each other to explain the reason for their visit.

'We've received new messages,' the councillor says.

'From the visitors from space,' Ender adds.

'Instructions for making contact,' the councillor says.

'For a meeting,' Ender explains.

'Look,' the Near Easterner says, although he should really have said 'Listen', as he now takes out his phone and makes as if to play Gastón an audio message.

Gastón looks behind him impatiently, as if he is worried that in his absence someone will swoop in and bury Kitten behind his back.

'Are you going to let us in?' the councillor asks, unaccustomed, unlike the Near Easterner, to being denied entry, to being met with suspicion.

'What does all this have to do with me?' Gastón replies, aggressively, transforming for a moment the flood of sadness hormones into anger, into animosity towards the two men.

The councillor reaches out his right arm and points behind Gastón, towards a spot that seems vague to us and, for a second, we fancy we see a spaceship floating above the market garden, just at that moment, like some kind of proof; but the councillor is pointing towards something specific.

'Is that a carob tree?' he asks.

'Here it is,' Ender says, holding his phone out to Gastón.

'I don't have time for this,' Gastón says brusquely, and turns his back, resolved to walk away.

He takes two, three, four steps, heading for Kitten's body, back to his mourning, listening to the two men's protests as they try to stop him.

'It's here!' the Near Easterner yells. 'The meeting's here!'

'Didn't you want me to help you?' the councillor calls out.

Gastón halts his departure to weigh up the situation. So many things have happened since his visit to the councillor that the plan they discussed then now seems like it came from another story, from something that happened to another person, in another life. Would he be able to convince Max to stay? How much would it cost to pay off all his friend's debts and build another restaurant? It seems an unlikely theory at this point, a fantasy of happiness that has slowly been crushed, in just a few days, in just a few pages. Is there a solution?

'Is that a carob tree?' the councillor asks again, seeing Gastón wavering.

'I'm not interested anymore,' Gastón replies, but he goes back to the spot where he has been listening to them, making it clear that he has doubts.

The councillor explains that all the signs indicate that the meeting place is Gastón's market garden, and that the carob tree is definitive proof.

'There are quite a lot of carobs around here,' Gastón says. 'It's a very common tree in the city.'

'The whole thing is like a riddle,' the councillor replies. 'We've ruled out all other possibilities and, in the end, your market garden was the only place left.'

Before Gastón can say a word, the councillor sets out his proposal. He looks to left and right, taking care that no one in the street can overhear him, making it clear to us that you cannot be too careful.

'You can't just come to the office to ask for something like this,' he says, lowering his voice, 'that's not how things work around here. You have to be discreet. Now I'll have to request that your name be erased from the calendar in the visitors' database on the computer. We'll need to wait a little so that anyone in the office who might have seen you forgets your face. But don't worry, it's just a question of time. You have my word.'

The councillor pauses, looks directly at Gastón, seeking his complicity; he comes closer to the gate, grabs hold of two of the bars with his hands and puts his face through the gap, towards Gastón.

'All we ask is that you let us in on the day of the meeting,' he says.

'I'm not interested anymore,' Gastón says again, and he turns his back on them and leaves them talking among themselves.

68

Gastón interrupts his digging to open the gate for the sedatoress. What with so many things going on, he forgot to let
her know, or perhaps this forgetting was not entirely involuntary: perhaps he was scared she would never come back,
now that the reason for her visits is lying among the roots
of the carob tree, half under the earth.

How will the sedatoress react? If this were a romantic story,
we would doubtless be reaching the climax, the moment
when Gastón and the sedatoress's feelings are revealed to
each other. It isn't possible to know yet, though, if there
is anything beyond camaraderie, beyond the sympathy he
inspires in her and the curiosity she sparks in him (although
it has to be said, relationships have been embarked upon
with much less than this).

The sedatoress stays where she is, at the half-open gate,
when Gastón tells her the news. She doesn't move forwards
to give him a hug, or stretch out an arm to place a patronising
hand onto a grieving shoulder.

'Have you buried him?' she asks.

'I'm doing it now,' Gastón replies.

'Can I keep you company?' the sedatoress asks.

Gastón nods and together they walk down the path
towards the carob. The sedatoress does not interfere with

the funeral task, but simply sits down and leans against the tree, watching Gastón shovelling earth to fill in the hole. The earth falls down onto Kitten's body; now the animal will be food for the carob, for its sweet berries which Gastón will turn into herbal infusions and remedies.

When he's finished, he puts down the shovel, wipes his hands on his trousers and sits down opposite the sedatoress. Like a sign that spring is on its way, today the sedatoress is wearing a pair of leather sandals; Gastón looks down at her feet for a moment, the second toe longer than the first, a hallmark of classical beauty, and sees the yellowish toenail. He looks up at her face, at the spider vein that now seems to him like a labyrinth, or maybe the thread to find your way out; a tangled path like the plot of this story, and we all know what the ancient philosophers used to say: that the labyrinth is an image of the soul.

'Don't take offence,' Gastón says.

'Don't say something offensive, then,' the sedatoress replies.

'I'm going to give you something for that toenail,' Gastón says. 'It's a gel I make with the green berries from the tree,' he adds, raising his eyebrows up towards the carob's branches.

'What's wrong with my toenail?' the sedatoress asks, defensively.

'Nothing,' Gastón says, and stretches out his right hand towards the sedatoress's foot.

His index finger touches the yellowish surface, stroking it, tracing the outline of the nail, and the sedatoress blushes so much that the spider vein disappears from her cheek.

69

He hasn't forgotten that he ought to ask the Far Easterner for help, but something has changed; these precautions now seem stupid to him, a frivolity one might permit oneself in other times, as if they have ceased to be important, but he is wrong, because the older man intercepts him before he can get to the shutters of the restaurant. The fact that Kitten's death has changed his perception of reality, of the emergencies and threats he is facing, has not, unfortunately, forced a change in reality itself, that obstinate, tedious thing. Gastón looks at the man resignedly, presuming, in a bored sort of way, that the time to confront him has come. He indicates the bar with a brief jerk of his chin, and the older man follows him obediently.

Gastón orders a beer, and the older man a sparkling water.

'I always treated him like a son,' the older man says. 'I invested a lot in him.'

The sentimental tale has no effect on Gastón now; it's too late for empathy or sympathy, and the older man's change of tack is useless. He talks of Pol's talent, of his intelligence, of his rigour in the lab, but also of how his lack of stability damaged his output; he mentions his shortcomings, his tendency to feel attacked and persecuted, and to shift blame onto others; his anxiety attacks, the risk of mental imbalance; and says that all of this, in some way, is due to his being left without a mother at a young age, when she died.

'Or having too many fathers,' Gastón replies, although he is actually saying something else, something worse: that we are the ones who have sent Pol mad, this fiction of men.

His tone is caustic, but the older man isn't even listening, or if he is, he is ignoring him; he has gone days without sleeping, waiting, and now he can't stop. He says that the way Pol abandoned his job was completely unjustified, and that he must pay back the investment that was made in him; his contract is tied to results, his pay is performance-related, and what he has been paid is not a salary, but a bonus based on results, which have not materialised. He then ventures a metaphor about Pol's behaviour, comparing him to a bacterium that only reproduces when it feels threatened; he talks of the Tundra, of the days without light or warmth from the sun, of the rate of desertion among researchers at the institute, a suicide that happened, alcohol abuse, pills and other substances.

'What is it that you want?' Gastón interrupts. 'Money?'

'There's something else,' the older man responds.

He takes a drink of his sparkling water and moves his head closer to Gastón, across the table.

'Pol has taken something,' he says, in a low voice.

'Taken something,' Gastón repeats.

'Yes,' the older man says; 'well, stolen.'

'What is it?' Gastón asks.

'I can't tell you,' the older man replies.

He explains that the investigations in the Tundra are confidential, that the results are the property of a group of investors, and that he cannot divulge this information without their consent.

'It's sensitive material,' he concludes.

'Sensitive,' Gastón repeats.

'Sensitive,' the older man says again, this time not clarifying the meaning of the euphemism.

Gastón finishes what's left of his beer, takes a few coins from his trouser pocket and places them on the table.

'I don't know where Pol is,' he says.

'I'm not asking you to tell me the truth,' the older man replies. 'I've got children, I'm not naive.'

'What do we have to do, to get you to leave us in peace?' Gastón says, including, with the use of the plural, Max and, even though he doesn't want to give himself away, Pol.

'Just make sure that Pablo doesn't use it,' the older man says. 'The material,' he clarifies.

He explains that in a couple of days he will have to return to the Tundra; he can't stay any longer, and if he doesn't find Pol he will have to lie, to cover up what's gone on, because otherwise he would jeopardise the trust the investors have in him. Gastón breathes a sigh of relief: he has just understood that the older man's fate, his career and all his projects, depend on Pol. This is why he has personally taken charge of looking for the boy and no one else has got involved (not the authorities, not the police, not anyone), because whatever it is that's happened must remain a secret. And it's not even a conspiracy – this is just what best suits the interests of the older man, who, because of negligence or a lack of supervision, is partly to blame for what has happened.

Gastón pushes back his chair, stands up and pulls on Kitten's phantom lead, shocked at how light it feels; then he walks out of the bar and crosses the road to the restaurant.

70

They're watching a match played by the city team and having a second beer at the bar of the empty restaurant; Max and his father on the barman's side, Pol and Gastón on the customers' side, Kitten's definitive absence at Gastón's feet, lying between two stools and rising up his legs like a chill until it lodges itself in his stomach.

'What if it was the sedatoress?' Pol asks.

He says that she could have slipped into the market garden when Gastón wasn't there, to put the dog to sleep once and for all. That she might have done it out of pity, so Gastón didn't have to go through it all. Once again, he is employing the logic of paranoia, where everything has an explanation and there is no room for chance. Gastón replies that he has seen too many films, bad ones, he stresses, and that it was just a coincidence, an unfortunate one, he adds, that he wasn't there at that moment to be with Kitten when he died.

The screens show that the best footballer on Earth has stopped running. He is bent over, his hands on his knees, spitting, or maybe vomiting. We watch him look out towards the edge of the pitch, over at the sideline to the left (where the coach is watching him carefully, his arms crossed and a worried look on his face), then straighten up again and wave his arms to ask to be taken off.

Gastón watches as the best footballer on Earth walks off the pitch, and he realises that this is the last time they will all watch him together, that Max's decision is going to break the cycle, the routine, all of those gestures repeated thousands of times for so many years, the calendar marked up twice a week for a match, the pretext for their get-togethers.

'You see?' Max says to Pol, looking up for a moment from the multicoloured sweeties. 'It's time to go home.'

It's the continuation of a previous chat, in which neither Gastón nor we have participated, although the context is enough to understand (and bemoan) the poverty of the meta-phor, the opportunism with which Max is appropriating the anxiety attack of the best footballer on Earth to suggest that it's a sign of how life in the city is degenerating. Someone else who might misuse the situation, Gastón reflects, is the North Easterner, who right now must be grumbling away to himself in the stands, interpreting what is happening on the pitch as a bad omen for the welcome he prepared for his brother.

Max's father stares intently at Gastón; he's not taken his eyes off him for several minutes now. The man cannot bear uncertainty, nor does he wish to humiliate himself by asking about the money in front of his son and grandson. Gastón feels the wad of notes in his pocket and doesn't take his eyes from the game; he likes having Max's father at his mercy; he plans on making him suffer until the last minute.

'Who are they sending on?' Pol asks.

The best footballer on Earth claps towards the stands, shakes the referee's hand and embraces the teammate who is trotting onto the field to replace him. He does all this so ceremoniously, so sorrowfully, that he seems to be saying goodbye to this story, too. Gastón and Pol yell the same insult, an insult which recalls the mother of the coach of the city team (or not exactly *his* mother), at the moment they discover who the sub is.

71

As he's leaving the restaurant, when the shutters are already halfway through their descent, Gastón sees El Tucu. He's leaning against the wall on the other side of the road, surrounded by the smokers who have just emerged from the bar on the corner to have a cigarette after the end of the match. He's holding a bottle of beer in one hand and cursing loudly under the balcony three floors up that has a municipal banner hanging from it, addressing late-night revellers in the native language: 'Be quiet – we're trying to sleep.'

Gastón greets him with a nod; more than a greeting, it is a gesture to let El Tucu know that he has seen him, is not ignoring him, and plans to slip away back home, but El Tucu crosses the road and intercepts him.

'Where's the dog?' he asks.

'He's at home today,' Gastón says, not wanting to give the man an explanation (and having no reason to do so, either).

El Tucu drains the last drop of his beer.

'Buy me a drink,' he says. 'I need to talk to you.'

We see him stagger slightly, wobbling from right to left with the swaying motion alcohol imparts after a certain limit is overstepped. Nothing good can come of this change in mood – this hyperbole of emotions – that distorts feelings. Gastón tries to make his escape.

'I'm going home,' he says. 'I've got to get up early tomorrow.'

'You can give me a job,' El Tucu says.

Gastón tells him that he doesn't need anyone, that he can look after the market garden by himself.

'If I don't have a work contract I can't renew my resident's permit,' El Tucu says.

'I don't need anyone,' Gastón insists.

'Just the contract, then,' El Tucu replies, 'so I can renew it while I look for something else.'

'I'm sorry,' Gastón says, and tries to move away, but El Tucu blocks his path.

They are face to face, bellies touching, and El Tucu starts breathing heavily, sending out telepathic insults. If we could go inside his head, we would understand the workings of this age-old resentment which has been the driver of so many summary executions.

'You'd have to pay social security, and if I got inspected the fine would ruin me,' Gastón explains, frightened.

'But you are going to hire that nutjob Pol,' El Tucu says.

'What?' Gastón says.

'He told me,' El Tucu says.

'Kitten's dead,' Gastón replies, distracted by thinking about Pol, about the possibility that the boy might stay with him, as if he were now replying to El Tucu's first question and this made it possible to start again, to rewrite the entire dialogue, to steer it towards somewhere other than this confrontation.

But El Tucu is not in the mood for revisions, rewrites or edits.

'Are you trying to make me feel sorry for you?' he replies, practically shouting. 'Or are you asking me to be your dog?'

He shoves Gastón angrily, more to get him away from him than to start a fight; Gastón seizes his chance and turns round, pulls on Kitten's phantom lead and runs off in the other direction, although he will have to go the long way round to get home.

72

The latest diagnosis is oesophagitis, Gastón reads on his phone, once he's in bed. The sports press has published a supposed medical report from the club, which hasn't been officially confirmed or denied yet. Oesophagitis causes acid reflux, nausea, vomiting and, due to the physical exertion involved, a feeling of choking, of extreme distress. The associated chest pain, they claim, is very similar to that felt during a heart attack. He also reads the rumours about signings and transfers for the next season, blacklists of guilty parties, cruel or patronising interpretations of the reasons that might explain the city team being knocked out of the continental championship.

Gastón shuts the browser and sends a message to the North Easterner: 'I'm going to need you to help me tomorrow. I'll come by first thing.' Then he messages Max. He asks him whether he's asleep, says to call him. Gastón sees on the screen that Max has read the message but is not replying. He waits for two or three minutes, then decides to get the ball rolling.

'Is something wrong?' Max asks when he picks up.

Gastón says that he wanted to ask him once more if he's sure about what he's going to do, that he should stay, that he, Gastón, can help him start again. Max thanks him and replies that if it's about starting again then he would rather do it where everything began, in his homeland. Gastón gives a disjointed reply, getting into a muddle as he tries to explain something, the gist of which, as far as we can tell, is that starting again while looking forwards, towards the future, is not the same as going backwards to start again while thinking about a lost past. That time is something you cannot get back.

'What have you got to do with all that, anyway?' he insists.

'All that' is what Gastón calls Max's homeland, his aunts and uncles, his cousins, nephews, nieces and half-siblings, who, after so many years, are just strangers; it's what he calls the nostalgic idea of a future in which Max plans to restore his childhood, to edit it, to live it now in a happy way.

'Pol's insisting on staying,' Max says.

He is steering the conversation towards a pending matter, asking for Gastón's help and letting him know at the same time that there's no going back from his plan, that it's a plan to go back you can't back out of.

'He says he can stay with you for a bit while he decides what to do,' Max says, 'and he can help you in the market garden. I'm worried the move might destabilise him even more – Pol needs to feel calm so he can get better.'

Pol could be a stand-in for Max; Gastón doesn't see it this way, but we realise that this is what's happening in the background: the start of a story, a fantasy that gives Gastón hope, hope that he won't be left alone, that he, too, will begin a new life, with Pol by his side, needing his care and his protection to get better, to recover from the difficult phase he's going through. Pol is not mad, no; if anything he is just as unbalanced as all the young people his age are, as anyone would be who, when they come out into the world, finds only wreckage, ruins, all promises unkept. He needs routine, normality, large doses of reality, concrete things to keep him occupied, to build a dam that will protect him from paranoid fantasies. The market garden is the perfect place, with its cycles, the regular attention it demands, the daily contact with the earth – this is what might save Pol. He could even let him do experiments, Gastón thinks, going out on a limb, could take advantage of the boy's knowledge of biology, improve his crops' productivity. It's vital to help him forget about conspiracy theories, it's vital to cultivate the market garden.

'Gastón?' Max says, thinking the line's gone dead.

'He can stay with me for the time being,' Gastón replies. 'If it doesn't work out he can catch up with you a bit later,' he adds, prudently, to emphasise that, at the end of the day, nothing in this life is final.

Gastón waits for Max's answer. Even though we can't see him, we can sense Max at the other end, hesitating, calculating, trying to select the right words.

'With Mum or with Dad,' he says.

'Eh?' Gastón says.

'I mean it sounds like we're trying to decide whether a child should stay with its mother or father,' Max replies.

Although he finds this comparison rather childish Gastón says nothing, because he knows that this is how Max is telling him that Pol will in fact stay, that he, Max, will not force his son to follow him in his plans, that at the end of the day he is an adult.

'I'll come and get you,' Gastón says.

'I'd rather take a taxi,' Max says.

'I'm going to take you to the airport,' Gastón says, firmly. 'I don't want to argue about it. Have you finished clearing the house? Or will Pol and I have to finish sorting that out?'

'I spoke to the North Easterner,' Max says.

'He's called Niko,' Gastón replies.

'He's going to keep the house, too,' Max says, 'for his brother's family. I sold him all the furniture, the crockery and everything. We agreed on a sublet.'

'That's illegal, Max,' Gastón says.

'I can't lose any more money,' Max replies.

'When was this?' Gastón asks. 'Why didn't you tell me?'

'Pol's right,' Max says; 'we sound like an old married couple. A married couple who don't talk to each other.'

Suddenly, Gastón is overcome, his cheeks grow hot and his tear ducts receive a warning signal: here come the sadness hormones. In thirty years they have never had to say these things to each other, ever; their friendship is made up of unspoken words, of euphemisms, of barbed jokes, of gestures repeated thousands of times, of everything that saved them from having to talk seriously about things.

'Did you lend my father money?' Max asks.

Gastón doesn't answer; he is still trying to summon his indifference hormones to do battle against this expected sadness.

Gastón allows himself to be amused for a moment by the image of Max's father fleeing, like in a film; he visualises him hidden beneath a hat and a long raincoat, and we see him in black-and-white, as if his escape to the tax havens of the Central West were taking place in the previous century.

'He gave me some of the money you lent him,' Max says, taking for granted Gastón's responsibility for the matter, 'for my expenses. He's a real maniac, my father. Always wanting me to be permanently in debt to him.'

73

Perhaps we shouldn't recount this, betray the trust Gastón has in us, alert the Peninsular fiscal authorities, but we have a greater responsibility. We were given a power to write this story and we must exercise it.

Gastón makes a call first thing in the morning, taking advantage of the time difference between where he is and the Southern Cone, of the fact that he's further ahead in time. The man he is speaking to is a lawyer, an old acquaintance (we deduce this from the way they greet each other, familiar and distant at the same time, which leads us to sense a long-standing relationship and an unswerving mutual understanding). Once they have re-established contact with a few preambles, Gastón tells the man that he needs to sell everything.

'Everything?' the lawyer asks.

'Everything,' Gastón replies. 'Right away, as soon as you can do it.'

'All right, but we'll need paperwork, signatures, powers of attorney,' the other man replies.

'Send me whatever you need,' Gastón says, 'but be quick.'

The lawyer tells him that it's not the best time to sell at the moment: there's an economic crisis (another one – what's new?) and it's more of a buyer's market, and it would be better to wait until there's a more favourable outlook, but Gastón carries on, telling the man which of his accounts to transfer the money to, and it's not an account on the Peninsula, it must be located in one of those tax havens in the Central West, maybe even the same one Max's father is headed to right now.

'Listen,' the lawyer says, 'do you not want to keep anything? A house you can come back to, at least, if you decide you want to come back?'

'I want you to sell it all,' Gastón insists, tersely, and he moves the phone away from his ear and presses the icon on the screen that ends the call, as if the past were something we could simply swat away (with the help of a lawyer).

74

As soon as Gastón pulls into the passenger pick-up and drop-off area, Max opens the door and steps down onto the soil on which he has lived for more than thirty years and which he is about to leave for ever. He wouldn't let Gastón park the van in the car park and is making him avoid a melodramatic farewell; he wants to speed up this chapter, as if an ellipsis could somehow alleviate the pain. Gastón gets out as well, to open the rear door and help carry the suitcases.

Pol gives his father a brief hug and tells Gastón that he'll be back in a minute, he won't be long, and not to move, and runs off before either of the two men can ask him anything.

The suitcases are already stacked up on the trolley that Max will use to push them over to the airline's desk; Gastón shuts the rear door of the van and walks over to Max, who is checking that he has his passports and all the flight details.

As they are about to give each other a hug, a policeman appears and asks to see the licence for the van. He tells them that this kind of vehicle isn't allowed in this part of the airport and starts tapping the details of a fine into an electronic device. Max tries to explain.

'It's no use,' the policeman says, cutting in.

'What?' Max asks.

'Trying to make me feel sorry for you because you're saying goodbye,' the policeman says. 'I don't know how you sort these things out in your homeland, but we obey the law here. Please don't say anything that might make me file a report for attempted bribery.'

Gastón realises that Max is about to wave his Peninsular passport in the policeman's face and so, to prevent this, he embraces him, whispering that it's not worth the hassle and carefully pushing Max's hand down towards his pocket to make him put the passport away. Today at least, as proof that something is ending or, rather, for Max, that something is beginning, his friend has had a shower. He has also chosen, from among the mounds of dirty clothes, those which were the least wrinkled and pungent.

'There's no rush,' the policeman says. 'Take your time.'

They finish their hug, and Gastón opens the front passenger door to take out the licence from the glove compartment.

'Where's Pol?' Max asks.

'I don't know,' Gastón says.

The two of them peer over in the direction they think Pol went, but they're not certain. The mass of tourists crowding all the entrances to the airport makes looking for him difficult. Max gives a little shrug to announce that he's leaving.

'Let me know when you get there,' Gastón says.

'Yes, Mum,' Max teases.

He starts to push the trolley with the suitcases on, heading over to the nearest entrance; we see him cross this page, leave the margins, and move off, out of Gastón's sight, of our perception.

Gastón waits for the policeman to do his job, and as soon as Max has disappeared completely, as if the airport were a great theatre, Pol enters the stage.

'What's that?' Gastón asks him.

He's carrying a hiking rucksack, a cylindrical one, or rather, one that's bulging in the shape of a cylinder because of whatever it contains.

'I dropped it at left luggage the day I arrived,' Pol says, 'I couldn't carry everything.'

'What is it?' Gastón asks, when he notices the strange shape of the bag.

'Things,' Pol replies, and he opens the passenger door and sits down with the rucksack on his lap.

75

At nightfall, the contactees appear in the market garden; for a secret society of conspiracy theorists, they really do make quite a lot of noise: they are shouting out to Gastón from the other side of the gate. Gastón thought he had dissuaded them, but he has underestimated quite how fanatical they are; he is sitting in the shade of the tool shed with Pol, drinking an infusion of carob leaves in an attempt to soothe the boy, who seems like he is on the verge of another nervous breakdown.

He pauses as he wonders where to start explaining to Pol what is going on, but Pol stands up and asks for the keys.

'I called them,' he says, holding his upturned hand out to Gastón.

Gastón doesn't move and looks from Pol to the gate, where we behold preparations for a mutiny; there must be around ten people altogether, and they are now shaking the gate violently.

'I didn't tell you everything,' Pol says, 'I'm sorry; I couldn't.'

Pol's outstretched hand is still waiting for the keys, and it reminds Gastón of those afternoons when he used to go and collect him from school, at five o'clock; the boy's palm held up to receive his afternoon snack, the other held out towards

Gastón so they could walk together to football practice or over
to the Square of the Revolutionary Women, hand in hand.

'Now you'll understand everything,' Pol promises.

There is a gleam in his eyes that we assume must be the
same one thousands of writers have described as the hint
of madness, or that trope so often trotted out in paranoid
fiction: that there is no clearer sign of the supernatural than
something strange in the eyes. Gastón doesn't give him the
keys; he stands up without a word and walks up the path to
the gate, with Pol following after him. The councillor and
Ender are there at the front, as well as Pol's old schoolteacher
who, although he is in theory the leader of the society,
stands a little way back, like a powerful man preceded by
his flunkies.

Before they reach the gate, Pol steps off the path and we
see him heading for the delivery van. He opens the passenger door, takes out the cylindrical rucksack, puts it over his
shoulder and starts walking back towards the gate. He goes
over to Gastón and unclips the keyring from his belt loop.
The contactees have grown calm at the sight of Pol, who is
searching through the bunch of keys, trying to find the right
one. He removes the padlock, pushes the gate half open and
tells Gastón to make sure to lock it.

'Let's go,' he orders the contactees.

Gastón sees them walk down the path towards the carob
tree, docile, pacified, ecstatic, as if they have stepped out of
themselves; Ender, the councillor, the consular secretary,
the yoghurt factory man, and a few more who will remain
anonymous on these pages; they are carrying shovels, hoes
and picks as if they were farmhands hired to bring in the
harvest. Gastón hurriedly locks the padlock again and runs
down towards them (we need him down there, we can't stay

at a distance now, right when we're so close to unravelling the mystery).

The contactees have started digging behind the carob tree, the other side to where Gastón buried Kitten; they do so in a coordinated fashion, without having received any instructions, as if they've been trained. The only one not digging is the leader, who embraces Pol before the two men open the rucksack and remove a small metal tank. Pol jerks his head to indicate to Gastón that he should come over; he twists the lid of the tank, which now looks to us like a thermos flask, and a cloud of dry ice floats up towards the sky over the market garden, although it evaporates before touching the leaves of the tree.

'It's liquid nitrogen,' Pol explains, 'to preserve the seeds.'

'Did they give them to you?' the leader asks, using the native language.

'Well, I actually had to take them myself,' Pol replies, in the same language.

From inside the thermos, Pol extracts an elongated test tube in which we can see a greenish-looking substance.

'This is where a new life form will start,' he tells Gastón, going back to the colonising language. 'This will be mile zero of the colony.'

Pol hands him the test tube, its surface frozen, and it burns the tips of his fingers. Gastón feels the weight of it in his right hand – it's light, although indisputably real, no matter how much things in fiction aren't supposed to weigh anything.

'What is it?' Gastón asks.

'Alien bacteria,' Pol says. 'We'll sow them in a pond,' he explains, as he raises his eyebrows to indicate the place where the contactees are still digging.

'Pol – ' Gastón starts to say.

'You could have believed me,' Pol says, 'you and Dad, we didn't need to come to this.'

But where have we come to? Or to what? We have come, unfortunately, to a place of literalism, to a place we shouldn't even have let ourselves get close to, because now we're going to need an explanation. What is in the test tube? What is that greenish substance? Gastón wonders what the older man can have meant by 'sensitive material', and rather than believing in extraterrestrial life he is more inclined to think of rare chemical elements, radioactive matter, genetic experiments, transgenic seeds, hybrid organisms.

'You can't do this,' Gastón says; 'it could be dangerous.'

'The really dangerous thing,' interrupts the old teacher, 'is the idea that everything that comes from outside, anything alien, is a threat that must be eradicated. You know what that's called?'

Gastón says nothing, because he is waiting for an answer from Pol, not a speech from his old teacher.

'Universal fascism,' the old teacher says, answering his own question. 'This fantasy that we have to protect some supposed purity, an original, primitive order, to safeguard some sort of essence, traditions, a better past – which side are you on?'

Pol comes over and puts both his hands on Gastón's shoulders.

'You believe me now, don't you?'

Gastón puts a hand to Pol's cheek, gives him back the test tube and walks over to the tool shed.

76

'I've arrived,' we read on the screen of Gastón's phone, on the instant messaging app. 'You only took two days,' Gastón types, 'did you swim there? Where've you been?' 'Are you jealous?' Max replies. 'This isn't working,' Gastón writes, 'I think we should end it.' 'Is there someone else?' we read in Max's message. 'Is it the sedatoress?' 'Are you feeling better?' Gastón replies.

Max sends a string of identical emojis, the crying-with-laughter faces.

77

He walks into the restaurant because the shutters are up and the door wide open, as if the place were being ventilated. Inside, the North Easterner and his brother are sanding down the wood of the bar; they have taken down the peppers decorating it and, little by little, the surface is losing its green paint. Gastón says hello and Niko says something to his brother in a language we don't understand, although it's not hard to imagine that he's bringing him up to speed, explaining who this is.

In the doorway to the dining area, Varya appears. She is holding the wooden peppers in her hands and we realise she has been playing with them; battling her shyness, she shuffles over to where Gastón is standing. She says something to her father.

'She wants to know where the dog is,' the North Easterner translates without pausing as he rubs the surface of the bar with the sandpaper.

Gastón wavers for a moment, as he tries to choose the words he will use, but then he remembers that it will be her father who will give the child the news. He says, simply, that Kitten has died. The North Easterner pauses in his task, looks at Gastón and then speaks, taking much longer than he ought to if he was really transmitting the same information to his daughter. Whatever he has told her is working, because Varya reacts with indifference.

'Can I take her to get an ice cream?'

Niko performs his role as interpreter. The little girl smiles, and nods her head.

'We are alone.' 'We are not alone.' The two epigraphs to Juan Pablo Villalobos' novel, one supposedly from a song by celebrated Mexican *ranchera* singer-songwriter José Alfredo Jiménez, the other supposedly from the mouth of Fox Mulder, the alien-obsessed protagonist of 90s sci-fi series *The X Files**, are contradictory, and yet of course both true. We are human beings, one particular species, and yet our bodies are not single entities: millions of other organisms depend upon us (and we upon them), live on our skin and our eyelids and deep within our guts. The young, troubled Pol, almost physically alone out in the Tundra (and very much psychically alone in his own personal mental distress), helps to discover that humans are actually the product of alien colonisation – that we are not alone and never have been. Where do we end and these other beings begin? Why is it important to us to define that boundary, that border?

The epigraphs describe the human condition, too: each of us is floating through life, through this world, through the universe, as a solitary being, and yet we are inescapably social creatures and there is almost always an accompaniment of sorts, whether it is one we actively seek out via

* Both quotes are in fact invented – even before our possibly unreliable narrator enters the scene, we have an unreliable author!

friendship, romantic love, or perhaps a pet, or else an involuntary encounter, brushing up against another soul as we go about our daily lives, the contact altering us irrevocably. As well as its enjoyable nods to sci-fi, *Invasion of the Spirit People* is, in part, about that contradiction, and about how it is this inevitable, messy yet delicious contact between people, rather than where any of us might be from or what we do for a living, that makes us human.

The voice on the first page, the one that walks us through the novel, informs us – the readers – that 'we're going to accompany Gastón at all times, as if we were floating just behind him and had access to his feelings, his sensations, the flow of his thoughts.' Even when our protagonist Gastón might feel he is alone, we, the readers, will be with him in some way. He is alone, and yet he is not alone. This insertion of the narrator into the story right from the start marks the rest of the novel, one in which the relationship between writer (or narrator) and reader is more explicit than in any of Villalobos' other works. We are made aware early on of the artificial nature of what is to come, and yet simultaneously asked to suspend our cynicism and go along with the conceit; our interest is piqued even as the wizard behind the curtain creating the whole thing is revealed. And this narrator is not only very present and rather vocal at times (so that we are not alone, even if we are reading the book alone); they are also a pleasing mix of occasionally unreliable (as befits the tradition of omniscient narrators) and touchingly respectful: when Gastón is going through a particularly difficult experience, our narrator politely requests that we retreat because 'we have no right to be there now', and tells us – in a conspiratorial invitation to be an active part of the process – that 'we'll prove that, even when writing fiction, there is a moral and an ethical framework that must be respected.' Literature is not (created) alone.

I have been lucky enough to be a sort of floating head just behind all but one of Villalobos' novels. The translator is a sort of floating presence over the shoulder of any book she works on, accompanying the characters as they move through space and time, observing, participating in a way, separate yet connected, part of the microbiome of the work and its life in a new language. I was made especially aware of this while working on *Invasion of the Spirit People*. With his characteristic humour and ability to quickly pierce assumptions we have about social niceties and human interactions, Villalobos examines what it means to be other, what it means to be from 'elsewhere', what it means to accept someone who is different and the cost to us all when this acceptance is not forthcoming. It is an examination of neighbourliness, of xenophobia, and of the things (and people) that make us belong, and of the risks inherent in failing to recognise that borders, passports and accents can only tell us so much about a person – that someone's personhood resides in so much more than where they are from, or where we think they are from. The importance (and existence) of borders is deftly skewered in the novel, an idea which translators are perhaps even more acutely aware of than most, working as we do to bring books, authors and ideas across borders in a hopeful attempt to subvert them. We are part of the new life of a work, and the new work in translation is evidence that the work is not really bound by any borders, is not the product of one (a)lone mind.

I completed the first draft of the book in August 2020, six months into the global pandemic, and was working on the book for most of the UK's first lockdown, a floating head just behind the novel's characters. Max, Gastón, Kitten, Pol and the Sedatoress were also floating just behind *my* head, though, accompanying me as I coped with living alone during one of the most confusing, lonely periods I and so many others have ever lived through. I saw very few people during that time, but Gastón and his friends were always with me. Although *Invasion of the Spirit People* is set in unnamed city, it is clear to anyone who knows Barcelona at all that the Catalonian capital is the model for where the book's action takes place, although it might be any large European city experiencing both immigration from ex-colonies and a worrying rise in neo-fascism. I spent time googling Barcelona's pavement tiles so as to describe them accurately; I asked Barcelona-based friends about the geography of particular neighbourhoods in order to decide between saying 'up' or 'down' a certain street; I zoomed in on internet images of Gaudí's Parc Güell to get the right description of a certain perimeter wall. My memories of this research are now pretty much indistinguishable from memories of actually being in Barcelona in what I think are still being referred to as 'the before times'. In fact, when I now recall any of the books I have worked on, I realise that I remember not only what it was like to be working *on* them (to be sitting at my desk puzzling over a particular conundrum), but also, more poignantly now in a world irrevocably altered by Covid when travel is still restricted and dangerous for so many of us, what it was like to *be in* them, to be *there*, where they were set, even if it was only in my mind as I sat alone (not alone) translating.

During lockdown I acquired a pet – a kitten (now a cat) who would often sleep on my desk as I translated, a little less alone now than before. I did not name him 'Dog', although that would have been funny. I do sometimes call him Puppy, which makes me think of the dog in *Invasion of the Spirit People* called Kitten, whose name in Spanish is 'Gato' ('cat', as opposed to 'Perro', dog). The translation of this name had to be funny (i.e. it had to be the name of another animal, different and yet closely related in cultural terms, somehow, to the actual animal it named; it wouldn't have worked if he'd been called 'Chicken', say), but it also had to be tender. This is a tender book, perhaps Villalobos' most tender, and even I, as a dyed-in-the-wool cat person, have to recognise that the word 'cat' itself sounds quite hard, that harsh, voiceless velar plosive followed by a one-syllable rat-a-tat-tat-like sound, and the word ending abruptly in another hard letter, a 't', which brings the mouth towards closed as the tongue presses against the teeth to voice it with a slight exhalation of air, a short hiss like an angry stray trapped in an alley. 'Kitten', however, while it also starts with a hard 'c', is followed by the softer, more uplifting 'i', which makes your mouth open in a smile, and 'kitten' ends in the soft hum of an 'n', almost a purr; it is a diminutive and we therefore read it as cuter than a cat. I also wanted it to be two syllables to match those of 'ga-to', which helps rhythmically when the dog is being referred to by other characters. I cried when Kitten dies, not just the first time I read the book, nor just during the first translation draft, either. He is as real a character as any of the humans in *Invasion of the Spirit People*, and my feelings for him were enhanced by my being less alone thanks to my lockdown cat.

In a very real sense, I was also not alone while translating for another reason: as I worked, I was being accompanied, observed – another floating head! – for a friend's PhD thesis. Barbara (Babs) Spicer's doctoral project at the Open University involves a process-oriented and translator-centred case study, and she asked if she could observe me while I translated.

I agreed and, once a fortnight or so, Babs would video call me after I'd settled down at my desk and I would clip the phone with her face on it into the bendy plastic arm with a set of jaws at one end I'd bought for the purpose, twisting it round so she could see (and record) my screen as I worked. It was as if she was floating just behind me and had access to my feelings, my sensations, the flow of my thoughts . . . Babs made several video recordings of me typing up various sections of successive drafts, and also asked me questions about particular translation issues or strategies.

The process made explicit to me both my own working practice (never have I been so (self-)conscious about which words I have to look up and what confused notes I leave to myself in the margins!), but also how translation, too, is about relationships and the porous borders between people, no matter how solitary it might at first seem as an activity. At first sight, yes, I was largely sitting alone at my desk with only a book and a laptop for company, but at all stages of the translation I was making contact with other beings. Babs asked me to add to a diagram she had made called a 'network map' in which I recorded all the people, forums and organisations I contacted to ask for advice while working. I asked my dad, a retired surveyor, about terminology relating to how land is reclassified. I asked a friend who translates from Catalan about words such as *riera*, meaning a kind of dry water course but also used to describe a street or passageway. I asked attendees at the Goethe-Institut Glasgow's regular translation roundtable, the Stammtisch, what they thought about the translation of the potatoes, and I joined a Facebook group for gardening translators to ask about how *calçots* (or elongated onions) are grown. I purchased a new ambidextrous mouse to help with RSI, one recommended by a translator friend who works from Kurdish, and as I edited, I listened to various playlists suggested by the translator (and And Other Stories' very own publicist), Nichola Smalley, after I put out a tweet asking for rhythmic instrumental beats to work to.

This translation (any translation, any book, surely) is thanks in part to all of this collaboration, one that starts with the author, and moves to the translator, and encompasses readers, friends, colleagues, other books, researchers, strangers and pets along the way. We are alone. And yet we are not alone.

ROSALIND HARVEY
COVENTRY, OCTOBER 2021

Dear readers,

As well as relying on bookshop sales, And Other Stories relies on subscriptions from people like you for many of our books, whose stories other publishers often consider too risky to take on.

Our subscribers don't just make the books physically happen. They also help us approach booksellers, because we can demonstrate that our books already have readers and fans. And they give us the security to publish in line with our values, which are collaborative, imaginative and 'shamelessly literary'.

All of our subscribers:

- receive a first-edition copy of each of the books they subscribe to
- are thanked by name at the end of our subscriber-supported books
- receive little extras from us by way of thank you, for example: postcards created by our authors

BECOME A SUBSCRIBER,
OR GIVE A SUBSCRIPTION TO A FRIEND

Visit andotherstories.org/subscriptions to help make our books happen. You can subscribe to books we're in the process of making. To purchase books we have already published, we urge you to support your local or favourite bookshop and order directly from them – the often unsung heroes of publishing.

OTHER WAYS TO GET INVOLVED

If you'd like to know about upcoming events and reading groups (our foreign-language reading groups help us choose books to publish, for example) you can:

- join our mailing list at: andotherstories.org
- follow us on Twitter: @andothertweets
- join us on Facebook: facebook.com/AndOtherStoriesBooks
- admire our books on Instagram: @andotherpics
- follow our blog: andotherstories.org/ampersand

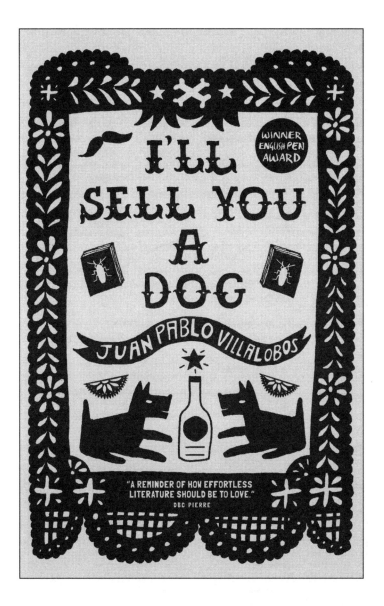

I'LL SELL YOU A DOG

JUAN PABLO VILLALOBOS

"A REMINDER OF HOW EFFORTLESS
LITERATURE SHOULD BE TO LOVE."
DBC PIERRE

CURRENT & UPCOMING BOOKS

JUAN PABLO VILLALOBOS was born in Guadalajara, Mexico, in 1973. He studied marketing and Spanish literature before working as a market researcher as well as writing travel stories and literary and film criticism. He has researched topics as diverse as the influence of the avant-garde on the work of César Aira and the flexibility of pipelines for electrical installations. His books include his *Guardian* First Book Award-shortlisted debut *Down the Rabbit Hole*, as well as *Quesadillas*, *I'll Sell You a Dog* and *I Don't Expect Anyone to Believe Me*.

ROSALIND HARVEY is a Fellow of the Royal Society of Literature, teaches translation at the University of Warwick, has served on the board of the Translators Association and is a founding member and chair of the Emerging Translators Network.